GOLDEN DEFENSE

There were three of them crouched behind the wagon. Skye Fargo. The girl, Pru. And the grizzled prospector, Sam.

Skye had counted at least fifteen men riding for them. Professionals by the look of them, with their trail-broken saddles and their range rifles.

One of their bullets hit the wagon. Skye heard a dull clink. It had hit one of the ingots piled high inside.

"Barrier's worth its weight in gold," Sam joked grimly.

Skye didn't have time to smile. He was too busy loading every gun he had.

Stacked gold wouldn't save them for long. Their only hope was flying lead—and lots of it. . . .

THE
TRAILSMAN

126

COINS
OF DEATH

by
Jon Sharpe

A SIGNET BOOK

SIGNET
Published by the Penguin Group
Penguin Books USA Inc., 375 Hudson Street,
New York, New York, 10014, U.S.A.
Penguin Books Ltd, 27 Wrights Lane, London W8 5TZ, England
Penguin Books Australia Ltd, Ringwood, Victoria, Australia
Penguin Books Canada Ltd, 10 Alcorn Avenue, Toronto, Ontario M4V 3B2
Penguin Books (N.Z.) Ltd, 182-190 Wairau Road,
Auckland 10, New Zealand

Penguin Books Ltd, Registered Offices:
Harmondsworth, Middlesex, England

First published by Signet, an imprint of New American Library,
a division of Penguin Books USA Inc.

First Printing, June, 1992

10 9 8 7 6 5 4 3 2 1

Copyright© Jon Sharpe, 1992
All rights reserved

The first chapter of this book originally appeared in *Blood Prairie*,
the one hundred twenty-fifth volume in this series.

 REGISTERED TRADEMARK—MARCA REGISTRADA

The Trailsman

Beginnings . . . they bend the tree and they mark the man. Skye Fargo was born when he was eighteen. Terror was his midwife, vengeance his first cry. Killing spawned Skye Fargo, ruthless, cold-blooded murder. Out of the acrid smoke of gunpowder still hanging in the air, he rose, cried out a promise never forgotten.

The Trailsman they began to call him all across the West: searcher, scout, hunter, the man who could see where others only looked, his skills for hire but not his soul, the man who lived each day to the fullest, yet trailed each tomorrow. Skye Fargo, the Trailsman, the seeker who could take the wildness of a land and the wanting of a woman and make them his own.

Denver City, 1860
where gold buys anything or anyone,
and greed can grind a man to dust. . .

1

The six-horse team was losing ground, hooves scrambling in vain on the loose rocks of the steep trail leading out of the arroyo. The stagecoach driver cracked the whip over the horses' sweating backs and their eyes rolled in terror, lips drawn back, mouths foaming on the metal bits. The team struggled to find a foothold, but still they slipped backward down the slope, dragged by the stagecoach which tilted on three wheels and slid precariously toward the edge of the gulch.

As he mounted the crest of the rise, Skye Fargo's lake-blue eyes took in the scene at once—the trickle of water which had carved the hazardous ravine out of the high plain, the steep rocky path leading down into and up out of the gorge, the trail washed out and treacherous by a recent cloudburst, the lost wheel of the coach lying below the trail on the rocks, the team sliding toward the cliff and the dusty brown stagecoach, sure to follow. Fargo heard a woman's scream from inside the coach as it lurched backward a few more yards.

Fargo put the spur to the Ovaro and the muscular horse surged forward beneath him, moving surefootedly and fast down the trail into the ravine, splashing through the trickle of water and climbing up the steep bank, shortcutting the trail which was blocked by the coach. Fargo seized his lariat and leapt to the ground beside a *pinon* pine, knotting the sisal rope quickly around the rough bark of the twisted tree—an old one with deep roots, he thought gratefully.

Fargo dashed toward the horses and looped the rope around the crossbar between the lead ones. As he was hitching the rope, the horses slipped again and the cord tightened across his fingers, catching two of them against the wooden crossbar. White pain flashed like sudden lightning. Fargo heard the awful sound of his own teeth grinding as he wrenched his fingers free of the tightening rope and it pulled taut.

One corner of the stagecoach already hung out in space over the gully. The door flew open. The passengers were panicking, Fargo thought. Any moment the ones closest to the door would make a jump for it, rocking the teetering coach and plunging it, along with the remaining passengers, over the edge of the cliff.

"Don't move!" he yelled above the whinnying of the team.

The sisal rope stretched, groaned once, then held. He would have to move fast. In an instant, Fargo eyed the heavy Concord coach—one ton of wooden joinery, iron, and leather. The team was jumpy. Any sudden movement would put an extra strain on the rope and it might snap, plunging the coach twenty feet down into the gulch. If one of the horses reared . . .

It wasn't over yet, Fargo thought as he strode toward the coach.

"Easy, easy," he calmed the team, touching the nearest ones on the necks and rumps as he made his way down the line. Now, if he could just keep the travelers calm and get them off the coach. There were two men on top, the driver and a grizzled prospector, by the look of his wide-brimmed hat.

"That was a close one," the greasy-haired driver said in a loud voice, wiping his face on his bandana. The stupid man seemed to think the coach was safe!

"Nobody move!" Fargo said.

He saw a woman's gloved hand grasp one side of the jamb of the passenger door and a female voice—a young one—said, "Hell's bells! Best thing is if we can jump down out of this contraption!"

Then Fargo heard another sound, a sound he didn't like half so well—the low groan of the rope holding the stagecoach to the *pinon* pine.

"Don't move!" Fargo yelled again, coming up to the coach door. Through the window, he saw a face—a pert upturned nose and brown curls under a straw hat, and a pair of thick horn-rimmed glasses.

"Saints alive! We need to get down outta here!" she said.

Fargo saw the coach rock as the passengers inside moved about and he heard a crescendo of voices babbling like a brook after a snow melt.

The driver stood up on top of the coach and started to climb down. "Sure was a lucky thing . . ."

Lulled by their sudden relief, none of them was listening to him, Fargo realized. He'd have to act fast.

"Freeze!" said Fargo, drawing his Colt revolver and aiming it in the general direction of the descending driver. "Damn you, freeze!"

The driver and the old prospector both stiffened and slowly raised their hands. The voices inside came to an abrupt halt.

"Just my luck," the old prospector muttered. "We don't go over the cliff. But we get held up by a bandit."

"One word, one move, and you're dead," Fargo threatened. They would be dead, or at least badly injured if they continued to panic and the rope broke. There was silence. The horses shuffled.

"Do what I say and no one gets hurt," Fargo said, turning toward the passenger door. Out of the corner of his eye, he saw the driver easing his hands down under the seat, probably to fetch his rifle.

Fargo wheeled toward him.

"You, get down," Fargo commanded the driver. There was no time for women first. Besides, he needed help steadying the horses.

"Hands up," Fargo said. "Leave the rifle on board. Move slowly. Do exactly as I say. One false move and the coach goes over the cliff."

As the driver stepped off the running board onto the trail, the coach gave another jolt.

"You next," Fargo motioned to the old prospector. "Move slow."

The old man climbed down, more nimbly than the driver had and more quickly than Fargo would have expected.

Fargo holstered his Colt.

"Now that I have your attention," he said, "get to the front. Keep the team quiet." He saw the surprise and relief on their faces. "If the rope breaks, keep the horses steady.

11

Without you two, the coach is lighter. The team should be able to keep it from sliding." He turned his attention to the passengers.

The pretty face in the window was all smiles. Fargo opened the door.

"Carefully, now. No sudden moves," he said, reaching up to lift her. He put his hands about her waist, a warm and rounded slenderness under a tight, fitted yellow bodice, which swelled and bloomed upward into high and fulsome breasts and downward into full hips under her blue riding skirt. Fargo lifted her easily and felt her wriggle slightly in his grasp. As he set her down, she removed her thick glasses and smiled. Her eyes were impossibly round and glossy brown, like her hair.

"Goodness gracious! Weren't we lucky you came along?" she said. Fargo smiled and turned back to the passenger door.

There in the doorway was a second girl, willowy and pale, as fragile as dawn, her long blond hair braided across her head and her eyes downcast. She was easing herself onto the running board, as if afraid to be helped.

"Allow me," Fargo said, reaching up to grasp her waist. She kept her eyes averted as he lifted her to the ground, noticing as he did that she was as weightless as a bird and she smelled of—he couldn't place it for a moment and then he had it—of lemons. Bracing. Fresh.

"Thank you very much," she said, smiling up at him shyly, then blushing and turning away.

Behind her, the last passenger, a graying man in a gray waistcoat, climbed carefully down from the coach.

"Paul Cavendish," he said advancing on Fargo and offering his right hand.

"In a minute," Fargo replied. "Let's get the coach hauled off this hair-raiser."

"Right," Cavendish agreed. "Tell me what to do."

"Brace the three wheels with rocks," Fargo said. "Wedge 'em in hard with a kick in case we start to slip." Cavendish did as he was ordered while Fargo hitched his Ovaro to the team.

When the wheels were braced, Fargo untied the lariat and quickly wound it, returning it to his saddle horn.

"You two get up the trail ahead of us," he commanded the two ladies, who quickly obeyed. "We don't want the coach rolling back over you if we lose it. You three men, go around to the back of the coach and hold up the rear end. I'll lead the team."

"Easy does it," he said softly to his Ovaro and to the horses, as he led them slowly up the rocky trail. Fargo kept the team moving slowly but steadily, until they gained the top of the ravine. He walked the team forward onto a flat section of the trail.

Fargo retrieved his lariat from the saddle. "I need one man to help me get the wheel," he said. The old prospector followed him down the trail, the loose gravel sliding under their boots as they descended.

The wheel lay on the steep slope below the trail, near the edge of the trickle of water.

"Wait here," Fargo directed him, handing him one end of the lariat. Fargo plunged down the slope, his muscular thighs catching his surefooted descent. He quickly knotted the rope through the spokes and ascended and the two of them hoisted the heavy wooden wheel up the rocky incline.

"There's your wheel," Fargo said, as he rolled it up over the top of the incline.

"Much obliged," the driver said. He had already fetched his toolbox.

"I'll help you," the prospector said. "I'm right handy with fixing." Together they bent to the task of fitting the wheel back onto the axle and replacing the main cotter pin which had jounced loose on the rough road.

Fargo unhitched his Ovaro from the team. He spotted a patch of tender shoots of bluegrass a short distance away. He led the pinto to the spot and put him on a long tether to graze.

Then the Trailsman straightened up to look around.

The high plains of eastern Colorado Territory rolled out in front of Fargo's eyes, with deep buffalo grass waving like ripples in a stream. The prairie was cut with deep gullies and dry canyons and gashed by dangerous ravines, like the one they had just come through.

This trail from Bent's Fort on the Arkansas River climbed

steadily, and emerged onto the high plain called the Divide. It was not the Great Divide, which lay along the spine of the Rocky Mountains to the west. This Divide was the high plain between the valleys of the Arkansas River to the south and the Platte River to the north where Denver City lay.

At the coach, Cavendish was giving his arm to the willowy young woman, helping her out of the hot late afternoon sun. The driver and the old prospector bent over the wheel. The brunette had raised a parasol and was twirling it slowly on her shoulder, first one way and then the other, walking toward him. Her horn-rimmed glasses were folded and hung on a thin chain about her neck. As she walked, the spectacles bounced against the dramatic curves of her breasts, the chain catching on one and then the other swelling mound.

Fargo put one finger to the brim of his hat as she approached. She nodded and smiled.

"What a beautiful horse," she said.

The pinto nibbled contentedly, moving among the sweetferns and the tender blades of spring grasses pushing up through the sod. His fore and hindquarter gleaned black and the afternoon sun illuminated the startlingly white band across his midsection.

"I've never seen a horse with those markings. What kind is it?"

"Ovaro," Fargo said. "A kind of pinto."

"Looks strong," she said, but her eyes moved, not over the pony, but over his own broad chest and tall, muscular body. She smiled appreciatively, bewitchingly.

"Rompin' rescues!" she exclaimed, her brown eyes twinkling. "Did I thank you yet for saving us back there? My name's Pru," she said, extending her hand as a man would for a handshake. "Short for Prudence. Not that I have much of that my daddy always said."

She looked him full in the face, chin raised, watching his face for a reaction, her cheeks blushing a little.

Fargo laughed. She certainly wasted no time.

"Skye Fargo," he said, taking her hand, careful not to grasp it too hard.

"Pleasure," she replied. She removed her hand from his and began to stroke the Ovaro's neck with long, lazy motions.

"What's a pretty woman like you doing out in Colorado Territory?"

"I'm heading to Denver City," Pru said, continuing to rub the horse. "I'm from Baltimore, but it's such a bore. Jumpin' Jimmies, the men there all play tiddlywinks!"

Fargo felt her eyes on him again in unabashed appraisal of his lean body.

"There aren't any men like you back in Baltimore. If it hadn't been for you, we'd have toppled into that stream. We'd be dead, or hurt at least. I was really serious when I said we were lucky you came by. I—all of us—owe you a debt," she said and paused giving him a searching look. "How can we, I mean, I repay you?"

"No need to," Skye said, smiling down at her. She raised her eyebrows slightly and her eyes sparkled.

"Maybe if I think real hard, I might think of something mutually agreeable," she said, twirling her parasol.

"I don't like obligations," he said. "But mutual pleasure is something else again." She giggled and blushed.

"It's highly unsual to see a lady traveling alone," Skye said. "What are you planning to do in Denver City?"

"Well," she said slowly, as if collecting her thoughts. "One thing is to find a job. I've got a great head for figures. At least my daddy always told me that. I used to work for him in his bank. In fact," she added, her voice taking on a note of seriousness, "you remind me a lot of him. Daddy was a good man—the kind of man you could trust."

Fargo waited, saying nothing as she paused. She looked across the empty plains as if she saw a far-off thunderstorm. Her face darkened. "You see, I worked for him when he was the director of the First Bank of Baltimore."

"And then?" Fargo asked.

She spoke softly as if through a gray haze of memory. "There was the flu epidemic. Mother died and he just couldn't get over it. Then he sent me away so I wouldn't catch it. I didn't get home until he had died too."

Fargo saw the tears standing in her eyes.

"And then my brother, he was trying to be like my father. But the bank fired him. He never told me why, but it just crushed him. And then he went to . . ."

Pru stopped as she saw Cavendish approaching.

"That was a nice piece of rescue back there," Cavendish said as he walked toward them. "Allow me to introduce myself formally. Paul Cavendish." He extended his hand and shook Fargo's vigorously.

"Skye Fargo."

Pru excused herself hurriedly and walked back to the coach, wiping her eyes discreetly with her lace handkerchief.

"Do you know how much farther we travel today?" Cavendish asked.

"You can reach Seventeen Mile House just about nightfall," Fargo said, referring to the next way station which was exactly seventeen miles from Colfax and Broadway in downtown Denver City. The network of stopovers, established by the stagecoach company, was named for the distance from the intersection of Denver City's two main streets. The stations spread out in a gigantic web on all the trails that led to the city and offered fresh horses and mules, water, fodder, and sometimes a hot meal and a place to sleep.

"What's the trail like from here on in?" Cavendish asked.

"Now that you've gained the Divide, it will be an easy time of it. All the way to Denver City. If the Indians cooperate."

Denver City. He felt the pull of it. Fargo caressed images of leisurely hot baths, some frilly female company, a couple of fancy meals, and maybe a few sharp and fast card games—a whole week of rest and relaxation, much needed after his last arduous trail.

"You heading to Denver City?" Cavendish asked him.

"Planning to," Fargo said.

Fargo turned and took the measure of Paul Cavendish—his neatly clipped graying beard and the smart gray waistcoat, gold watch fob looped across his chest, and shiny black boots. Cavendish's face was lined with concern, as if he carried a great weight on his shoulders. His gray eyes were steady, penetrating.

"This your first time in Colorado Territory?" Fargo asked.

"No," Cavendish said. "I'm from Boston originally. But I moved out to Denver City six months ago. I was just back east to bring my daughter Laurel to live with me. She's attended a girls' school in Boston since her mother died four years ago.''

"Pretty girl," Fargo said with a nod toward the coach, where the two women sat with the doors open to catch the afternoon breeze. "What are you doing in Denver City?"

"That was a nasty gulch," Canvendish said, changing the subject. "To look at this plain, you wouldn't expect these sudden ravines."

"Water runoff," Fargo said, wondering what Cavendish was hiding. "There's not enough ground cover to stop the snowmelt or the sudden spring showers, once the water gets going. This country's famous for flash floods."

"This is the first time I've been on this trail," Cavendish admitted. "I've gone back and forth a few times to Philadelphia, but always before I've traveled through Leavenworth, Kansas."

"That's the direct route from the east," Fargo said. "Why are you taking the long way around?"

"Just curious about the trail," Cavendish said, evasive again.

Fargo glanced over and saw that the wheel was replaced on the stagecoach. The old prospector was handing the tools up to the driver who was storing them in the box under his seat.

Fargo untied his horse, and he and Cavendish walked toward the coach. The prospector straightened up at their approach.

"Mighty obliged to you," he said to Fargo, extending a rough hand. "Sweeteye Sam's the name. Didn't catch yours."

"Fargo. Skye Fargo."

Sam blinked and removed his hat, revealing his grizzled hair matted down by sweat.

"Fargo, as in the Trailsman?" he asked.

Fargo nodded.

"As in *The* Trailsman?"

Fargo nodded again, noticing that Paul Cavendish had stopped beside the coach and had turned his head to listen to their conversation.

"I've heard some wild tales about you," Sam said

excitedly. "You seemed to have outfoxed every Indian, cougar, and bandit in the territories and broken more new trails than a herd of hungry jack rabbits. I'd like to talk to you, Trailsman. Maybe we could trade a few yarns. A fellow like me could use a few good tales to chew on while I'm panning."

"Why don't you ride with us to Denver City?" Cavendish asked. "I'd like to hear about your exploits too. And I want to talk over a business proposition. You might be just the man I've been looking for."

"Suits me fine," Fargo said. He looked at the sun touching the top of the peaks. "It's not far to the way station and if we move on now, we'll be having dinner there in a little over an hour's time."

Just as the coach was ready to roll, Pru opened the door and stepped out. She strode over to Fargo who stood beside his Ovaro.

"Bouncing boxes! I'm so tired of riding in that stuffy old coach, I could just spit. Do you think there's room for me up there with you?"

"Climb aboard," he said.

Pru placed a slender foot into the stirrup and Fargo caught a glimpse of lacy garters and shapely legs as she swung up onto the horse.

Then he swung up into the saddle behind her and clucked to the Ovaro. They moved slowly out in front of the coach, Fargo's muscular arms around Pru, holding the reins.

With every gentle sway of the horse Pru seemed to relax and melt against Fargo's broad chest. Even her back and shoulders felt soft, giving, like a cloud of cotton and her hair was warm and woman-scented. Words seemed to be unnecessary as they rode through the gradually darkening plain. Fargo was enjoying the closeness of Pru, her softness, her sweet smell, the sight of her tantalizingly curved breasts as he looked down over her shoulder. It had been a long trail and he was tired out, ready for anything that was not cold, dangerous, or uncomfortable. At least for a while.

After a few miles, in the distance she spotted a long low line of trees along one of the gulches.

"What kind of trees are those?" Pru asked. She raised

her arm and pointed—unnecessarily—and leaned against his left arm. He felt the warm full softness of her left breast press against his hard bicep. She remained there, her firm breasts rubbing up and down gently with the gait of the horse.

"Cottonwoods," he said, bringing his mouth close to whisper it into her ear.

He felt himself harden against the gently swaying warmth of her pressing up against him in the saddle. He felt himself swelling with desire, wanting her. She felt it too and shifted her rounded hips against him.

"Knocking nightshirts, Skye," she said, turning half around in the saddle, to catch his eye. "I'll bet you don't even know what tiddlywinks are!"

Fargo lunged and tightened his arms around her as she nestled into his chest. He watched her horn-rimmed glasses bouncing against her breasts.

Later, he promised himself silently. Later tonight.

As they rode the last few miles, Fargo could feel Pru's growing fatigue.

"Do you want to ride in the coach for a while?" he asked.

"I'll hold out," she said determinedly.

The sky was smeared with pink and purple clouds and darkness crept along the ground as they neared the Seventeen Mile House. The way station was a combination potato farm, inn, and stable.

The two-story farmhouse faced a wide yard with watering and feeding troughs, hitching posts, a long low line of stable stalls and a large barn. The door to the barn was open and golden light spilled out across the yard, illuminating a half-dozen people gathered around a mountain wagon and a gaudily painted cart with one flap down.

Fargo reined in the Ovaro and dismounted, turning to lift Pru down. He could tell Pru was tired out by the way she swayed when he set her down.

"Thanks for the ride, Skye. I think I'll freshen up and see you at dinner," she said, turning toward the house.

Fargo unhinged the bit and the pinto bent its long neck gratefully toward the deep clear water of the trough which reflected the last pale light of the twilight sky.

The stagecoach pulled in behind them and there was a flurry of activity as Cavendish and his daughter Laurel disembarked and the team was unhitched. Sweeteye Sam sauntered over to stand beside Fargo and they joined the knot of people standing in front of the mountain wagon to which was hitched the brightly painted cart.

The sides of the cart had been built up with panels to form a tall box. Colored flags flew from each corner of the box. On the side facing the yard, a flap of the cart was raised and painted on it in bright lettering were the words: MAXIMUS SWEEDLER, DOCTOR EMERITUS OF PHYSIC, PURVEYOR OF PATENT MEDICINES AND PRECIOUS SEA SALTS, LEECHES AVAILABLE. The open flap revealed shelves with rows of bottles filled with colored liquids and small paper bags wrapped with string.

Standing on a box was a rotund man, undoubtedly the Doctor of Physics himself, Fargo thought. Maximus Sweedler's bright green-striped suit fit him like the skin on a watermelon about to burst and his face was red with excitement.

"You there," Maximus Sweedler said, pointing straight at Sam, who jumped. "You, my venerable and undoubtedly august fellow, would appear to my practiced and trained eyes—educated at the very finest European universities as a fully authorized Doctor Emeritus Honorarium Superiorium of Physic—yes, you my fellow wanderer, are undoubtedly a prime candidate for the dreaded disease Emplympius Irreguli. I can see it in your eyes!"

Fargo and Sam traded sideways glances that said "How long will this sideshow be amusing?"

"Emplympius Irreguli!" Maximus repeated, shaking a pudgy finger in Sam's direction. "The symptoms are legion. Do you have a hard time falling asleep?"

"Never!" shouted Sam.

"But you do, yes, I know you *do* have a hard time staying *awake* late into the night!" Maximus insisted.

"Only if he's listening to your sales pitch!" Fargo said.

Several of the onlookers chuckled and applauded.

"And I would hazard a guess," Maximus continued, as if he hadn't heard the interruption, "that the skin around your nails is dry and your eyes smart after a day on the trail, both of which indicate the most egregious and sometimes fatal deficiency of veritosis!''

"How about *your* fatal deficiency of verity?" Fargo asked, and several onlookers laughed out loud.

"Yes, dear friends, I can tell from the color of this man's face that he will not walk among us in glorious God-given health. My friends, there is only one known cure, distilled from a rare lotus flower found only in the dark reaches of the upper Nile . . .''

Fargo shrugged at Sam and they moved away toward the stables, leading the Ovaro. Several of the other spectators followed them. They heard Maximus Sweedler's high voice reaching after them, "Don't turn your backs on a cure, my friends. This elixir is simply a miracle . . .''

Seventeen Mile House had a reputation for the best grub in the territory outside of Denver City. Fargo finished several plates of potatoes along with a rare steak, and washed it all down with homemade beer.

He sat at a wide wooden table with Paul Cavendish and Laurel, Sam, and Pru. Between stuffing his own mouth, Sam had plied Fargo with questions about his travels.

Pru listened to the stories, her brown eyes wide, and asking endless questions. Paul Cavendish also listened carefully. Fargo looked up several times to find Laurel staring at him. He smiled at her encouragingly, but she looked away.

"So, what's trailblazing *feel* like?" Pru asked Fargo, blinking her eyes.

"Feel like?" Fargo said, tasting the unaccustomed and unexpected word. "Blazing a trail through the wilds is like riding into the unknown future," the Trailsman answered, and he saw, for an instant, the lonely miles and the dangers that lay behind him. "It's never knowing what will jump you, shoot you, or fall on you next. You get so you can taste danger, smell it, feel it, a split second before it happens."

They were all silent for a moment. Pru turned to Sam. "And how's prospecting?" she asked, giggling and eager to change the subject to something lighter.

"A backache married to a dream," Sam said with a hearty

laugh. "Most of my days, I bend over in freezing snowmelt and pan. Or, if I find a good spot, I build a good sluice. That's a contraption that kinda speeds up the process. I personally don't much go for mines. A man can lose his soul down there in the dark of a gold mine. I prefer picking up the gold nuggets and washing away the sediments of the streams. The scenery's better."

As Sam began to relay a story about an early claim stake he had at Pike's Peak, Fargo let go of the sense of Sam's words and allowed the sounds of them drift around him as he studied the old prospector.

Fargo could spot a gold prospector a mile away and Sam had all the characteristics. It was more than the hat he wore, wide-brimmed to keep the beating sun off his shoulders during the long hours of panning.

In the light of the oil lamp, Fargo read Sam's face and found there the kind of hope most men leave behind in childhood. The kind of hope that gets children up early on Christmas morning to look for the apples stuffed into their woolen stockings. An innocent kind of hope that could drive a man to break his back, squatting in a cold mountain stream month after month, washing the sand away from the gold flakes.

That kind of hope was different from gold fever. Fargo had seen that too. Gold fever was a hard-edged glint in the eye. Fargo had seen folks infected by it, selling everything they had to buy mining equipment or a tattered map to some fabulous mine. Then they raced off into the arms of hostile Indians, hunger, and cold, with only the dream of gold to keep them going. The lucky ones returned empty-handed, but cured. The unfortunate ones found just enough gold to feed their fever and they spent years chasing the rumor of riches from one lonely stream or one hollow mine to the next.

Then there were the others, the dangerous ones. Fargo had seen them too, the men with bitter and hooded eyes, who burned for possession of gold, thought of gold, twitched in their sleep for gold, until the thought of gold burned away all else.

But as Fargo looked across the table into Sam's eyes, he saw no sickness, only hope. Sam's eyes crinkled when he grinned. He was grinning now, a deep wide gash in the middle of his grizzled beard.

"Don't you ever quit? Lay off!" Sam said, as the pudgy fingers of Maximus Sweedler fluttered over his plate of food, sprinkling something onto Sam's plate.

"The benefits of these precious sea salts are astounding my friends," Maximus said. "Note the pale gray color of this salt. This shows the presence of important minerals, vital to the body's well-being."

"Shove off," said Fargo, "and that'll improve our well-being." Maximus glanced nervously at the tall figure and began to stutter as he tried to keep his sales pitch going.

"These p-p-precious salts are imp-p-ported from the shores of the North China Sea . . ."

Fargo rose to his feet, a grim look on his face. Maximus looked up at him and his face flushed red, but he stood there stubbornly, one hand still holding the pinch of salt above Sam's plate. This was a man who never gave up, Fargo thought. If he weren't such a pest, he would almost be admirable. Maximus opened his mouth to start again.

"Getting a little late for sale pitches," Fargo said firmly, looking down at Maximus.

"What time is it?" Cavendish asked, drawing his gold pocket watch from his vest pocket. He looked at the face for a moment and then held it to his ear. "Seems to have stopped," he said.

"Please allow me," Maximus said, extending his open palm toward Cavendish.

Cavendish hesitated, holding on to the gold watch.

"No, no, you do not understand," Maximus said. "Wilhelmina! Wilhelmina!" he called out, looking around the crowded dining room.

Fargo saw an angular woman with auburn hair appear at Sweedler's side. Her sharp eyes glittered in the dim light and Fargo thought of a rodent—a sleek mink or weasel.

"Oh," she said, catching just a glimpse of Cavendish's watch. "A twenty-four carat Seth Thomas!" she said.

"Quite right," Cavendish said, impressed.

"My wife, Wilhelmina," Maximus said. "She can fix anything in just one moment. You watch and see." Fargo

23

noticed that Maximus's language was much simpler when he wasn't trying to sell his wares.

Wilhelmina extended her thin hand, her long bony fingers reaching for the golden watch which Cavendish slowly handed to her. She sat down at the table and from one pocket of her skirt drew forth a small flat wooden box, which she opened to reveal delicate tools.

She pulled the oil lamp closer to her and expertly removed the back of the pocket watch. Holding the complicated mechanism up to the light with one hand, she made deft adjustments with the other, using a screwdriver almost as thin as a wire.

"It is in fine shape inside," Wilhelmina said to Cavendish, "but one of the cogs had stuck—perhaps by a sudden shock to this watch?"

"I did drop it on the floor a few days back," Cavendish said.

"I will loosen it and it will begin to move again. Then it should give you no problem," she said. In another moment, she had replaced the back on the watch and handed it, ticking, to Cavendish. She put her tools away in the wooden case, as Maximus moved to stand beside Cavendish, his pudgy hand extended.

"How much?"

"Fifteen dollars," Maximus replied, "and a bargain for such fast, excellent work."

"Highway robbery!" Fargo said. "Pay a quarter-eagle. That's more than enough!" Cavendish flipped the small gold coin toward Maximus, who caught it in midair and examined it, holding it up to the light.

"What is this coin?" Maximus asked suspiciously. " 'Auraria Private Mint'?" he read off the coin face. "I've seen Conway coins and Parsons coins, but I never seen one like this."

He lifted it to his mouth and bit on it, then examined the tooth marks in the soft gold of the coin's surface.

"It's from the new private mint in Denver City," Cavendish explained. "I assure you, it's perfectly good money. We've just started minting them."

Fargo felt his ears prick up at the sound of the word "we." And Fargo was not the only one. Beside him, Pru gave a start and turned and looked at Cavendish long and hard.

Fargo had wondered why Cavendish had been so quiet about his own affairs, but now it made sense. A man who worked at a mint, if he was smart, didn't flash the fact around. But what was Pru's interest in the mint? Or in Cavendish?

Before he had time to wonder further, the innkeeper arrived with the bill. Chaos ensued as they tried to figure out what they owed.

"Mr. Cavendish, you never told me you work at the mint," Fargo heard Pru say above the hubbub. "What's it like there?" Despite the noise, Fargo caught the suppressed interest in her voice.

"Whatever gave you that idea?" Cavendish asked evasively.

"Oh, just something you said," she returned and her mouth opened to ask another question when Cavendish turned toward the Trailsman.

"May I have a word with you, Mr. Fargo? Outside?" Cavendish said, rising and pocketing his repaired watch. "Goodnight, my dear," he said to Laurel.

Fargo started to stand and then felt Pru's hand on his thigh under the table. Her touch went through him like a pleasant, warm wave. He turned toward her and she said quietly, under her breath, "I'm in Room Six, if you need some company. Later."

He smiled and rose, nodding Cavendish toward the front door. Outside, all was quiet. The stars winked overhead and the muffled, peaceful rustling of the horses in their stalls drifted over the yard.

"So, I gather you've got a job for me having to do with the Auraria Private Mint," Fargo said, as they leaned against a fence.

"That was a stupid slip of the tongue I made in there," Cavendish replied. "I've been director of the mint for six months. I've made it my policy to keep a low profile, especially when traveling. You never know who might be listening."

"That seems wise," Fargo agreed. "So, what's the story?"

"As you know," Cavendish said, "Denver City is a

magnet for every two-bit prospector and overnight millionaire within five hundred miles. Gold dust and nuggets pour in, but the stuff is hard to measure and spend in the raw form.''

"If you've got a flood of raw gold, it makes sense to get it converted into some kind of spendable, standard form as quickly as possible,'' Fargo said.

"Precisely. So, a few prominent citizens got together three years back and founded the Auraria Private Mint. It's legal in the territories to mint your own coins. The Auraria Private Mint does just that.''

"Nice business,'' Fargo commented.

"We turn a profit,'' Cavendish said. "But a modest one. Most of our gold is converted to ingots for shipment back east. About a year ago, we began minting coins on a limited basis.''

"You said you had only been in Denver City for six months . . .'' Fargo said.

"You forget nothing,'' Cavendish observed. "I came to Denver six months ago to take over the mint. The former director was caught skimming, taking a pinch here and there of all the dust flowing in. They never got enough proof to arrest him, but the board of directors felt sure enough of his guilt to fire him. And that's when I came aboard to straighten things out and rebuild confidence.''

"So, what's the trouble?''

"The flood of gold into Denver City just keeps increasing. The mint needs to expand. We have ordered a new coin press from the Federal mint in Philadelphia. We're planning to take a major gold shipment back east of $30,000 in gold ingots to pay for it.''

"And you want me to find a trail out of Denver for the gold shipment?'' Fargo said. "And that's why you were taking the long way back into Denver City—to scout out the southern route?''

Cavendish nodded.

"There's more,'' Cavendish said. "Just before I left Denver City, I got some information from a source that there's an ambush planned. I don't know who, how or when. But I've heard it's a big one—a lot of men, a lot of guns. It wouldn't matter how many men I sent out with the gold. The only way to get it through safely is to slip it through.

I need someone who can move silently and leave no trail—not break a blade of grass in passing—while hauling one and a half tons of gold! I need the Trailsman.''

"I was planning for a week of relaxing," Fargo protested.

"You can have your week. And it will be on me. Wine, women, and song—anything you want. After the gold shipment."

"I don't know if it's worth it to me," said Fargo. "I'm ready for some relaxation now."

"Well, we won't be ready to move the gold out for a couple of days. Enjoy yourself. I'll put you up in Denver City. But when we're ready, it has to travel safely. The mint can't afford to lose $30,000 in solid gold ingots."

"Sounds like a tall order. Give me some more details. Who's your source on the ambush information?"

"I'd rather not say," Cavendish answered.

"I need to know," Fargo said, "or it's no go."

"All I can tell you is that it's from a reliable source and that it's a lady in Denver City. I can't say more."

Fargo thought for a minute. "Okay, fair enough," he said at last. "Is this an inside job? How would someone find out about this gold shipment?"

"You ever tried to keep a secret in Denver City?" Cavendish asked with a chuckle. "It's the talkingest town I've ever seen—or heard. And I've got a board of directors with eleven mouths yacking that they just voted to buy a new coin press! There's no need for this to be an inside job. Everybody in Denver City knows the whole story."

"What's this job worth to you?" Fargo asked.

"Name your price," Cavendish answered coolly. "Just don't insult me by biting on the coins."

Fargo smiled and shrugged. He could have his cake and eat it too—a couple of days in Denver City, a lucrative job lined up, and then a whole week of relaxation all expenses paid. And he was beginning to think about the challenge of slipping one and a half ton of gold ingots out of a teeming city without anyone knowing about it. There were ways to do it. There were places he could hide his trail and no one could follow.

"Three thousand?" Cavendish suggested.

"Plus the week's expenses in Denver City?"

Cavendish nodded immediately.

"Sold," Fargo said. "We'll work out the plan in detail when we arrive in Denver." They shook hands on the deal and went inside.

"Come in, Skye," Pru's voice said from behind the door of Room Six.

"I heard there's a tiddlywink game going on up here," Fargo said as he pushed open the door.

Pru stood by the four-poster bed, her arm wrapped around one of the thick posts. She wore a white nightgown and her brown curls were brushed out. Her long hair fell thick around her shoulders and down her back, shining in the low light of the oil lamp beside the bed.

Fargo shut the door behind him.

"Waitin' widows!" she said, her eyes shining. "I thought you'd never come."

"I'm always up for tiddlywinks," he said, feeling himself stirring at the sight of her. The white gown did not conceal the hard points of her nipples, erect beneath the thin fabric. He began to slowly unbutton his shirt, keeping his eyes on her. He wanted some questions answered first.

"What's your interest in the mint?" Fargo asked her.

He saw Pru's face fall and the smile leave her mouth.

After an instant's hesitation, she said, "I was just surprised, that's all." Fargo felt sure that wasn't the whole answer.

He peeled the shirt off his muscular form and felt her eyes linger on his broad chest and his strong arms. He began to undo his belt buckle, but slowly, keeping his eyes on her.

"It was . . . it was just that Cavendish never said anything about the mint, the whole time we were riding in the coach . . . and . . ." Her voice faltered as she became distracted as he undressed. "And well, if Cavendish is working at the mint and I'm looking for a bank job, I thought I could ask him for work at the mint!" she said with a note of triumph at the end of her sentence.

Fargo knew she was hiding something. But now was not the time for more questions. He dropped his Levi's and his underdrawers and saw her eyes widen. He'd find out why Pru was so interested in Cavendish and the mint—but later.

2

In an instant, Fargo crossed the room and folded Pru into his arms, his mouth on her sweet hair, her warm neck and and then hungrily seeking and finding her full lips. Her mouth parted and he felt her tongue, seeking shyly at first, pointed and delicate. His hands were entangled in her long hair, moving down and sculpting her slender waist and then her round hips.

She unbuttoned her gown and he saw her plump breasts, rosy with the dark tips erect and eager. He bent his head and took one nipple into his mouth, teasing it lightly with his tongue, then faster and faster as he heard her breathing quicken.

"Yes, yes, oh, Skye," she breathed. With one hand he fondled her other nipple, moving his finger against the hard tip, faster and faster like his tongue, while with the other hand he brushed teasingly across her soft belly, downward into the short curly nap. Then he inserted one exploring finger into the warmth of her sudden wetness.

She cried out and shuddered as he touched her.

"Please, please, Skye. Yes, yes, I want you," she cried out, clutching the bedpost for support.

Fargo straightened and suddenly lifted her onto the bed. She moaned and writhed as his fingers kneaded her moistness. Her lips engorged, her dark tunnel pulsed with wanting. Fargo felt her hand close over him, and she gasped, her hand tightening, stroking, and he felt himself straining with yearning—yearning to be inside her.

"Yes," she murmured, "please yes." And he slid himself slowly into her waiting tunnel, feeling her tight, pulsating warmth around him. His tongue at the same time thrust deep in her mouth. He pushed again and again up into the tight warmth of her, until it was impossible to tell where he ended and she began—her mouth sucking on his lips, his tongue, and her tightness, pulling him as deep into her as was possible. She writhed and screamed under him, bucking up and down like wild horse.

"Yes, yes. Oh, God! Oh God!" she screamed, her panting louder and louder.

Fargo felt himself at the brink, but he held back, plunging into her slowly again and again, moving his muscular frame against her. He left her mouth and took one nipple gently between his teeth, teasing it again with his tongue while she screamed, bucking harder and harder until she suddenly shuddered violently. He plunged, the deepest into her tightness and gave himself to her, unable to stop now, shuddering himself, again and again until he was spent and he fell forward onto her.

She wrapped her soft arms about him and they breathed together, fast and then slower.

"Holy oysters," she said sleepily after a while. "There just aren't any men like you back in Baltimore." Fargo reached over and turned back the wick, extinguishing the oil lamp. She nestled up to him, her long hair a tangled darkness against the white pillow.

Fargo heard her breathing slip into sleep and he cradled her warmth against him.

After a while, Fargo heard Pru's breathing change and she moved uneasily from side to side. She moaned once and he heard her say, "It's not your fault, Don't blame yourself. It's not your fault."

Fargo gently shook her shoulder and she awoke, gasping, pulling away from him at first until she awoke fully.

"You were having a bad dream," he said gently.

"Oh, it was terrible," she said and he heard her sniff. Her voice sounded young and scared. "It was when Daddy was sick . . . and I was far away. I should have been there. I should have been there to help him."

She shivered, burying her head against Fargo's broad chest. He held her again, close to him, and she felt like a little girl as she grasped his hand, holding it close against her softness. He listened to her breathing deepen into a regular rise and fall. She was sleeping now, soundly, the bad dreams banished for the night.

She was brave in her own way, Fargo thought. Brave or very foolish. Fargo wondered what was driving her. Or calling her.

The room was stuffy and the thoughts whirled around inside of him like Pru's parasol in the afternoon sun, thoughts of gold ingots, Denver City, and the ambush conspiracy. He needed fresh air and the open sky to clear his mind.

After a long time, he slid out of the warm bed and dressed quietly. He silently descended the stairs and made his way across the yard, past Maximus Sweedler's mountain wagon and the painted cart, to the stable where he looked in on the Ovaro and fetched his bedroll.

The stars were bright overhead. He walked through the potato field, among the rows of young plants just coming up and rustling softly in the night wind. On a soft grassy patch under the rangy arms of a cottonwood, he stretched out his bedroll on the cool ground and looked up into the night sky.

Something pricked at his thoughts like a nettle. He thought again of Pru and the way she jumped at dinner and stared at Cavendish when he mentioned the mint. What was she hiding?

And Cavendish—Paul Cavendish had told him everything about the mint and the shipment, except where his got his information on the ambush. A little piece of information like that could make the difference between life and death—his own, Fargo thought uncomfortably. Cavendish had said the tip came from a lady in Denver City.

Well, Fargo thought, he would try to track her down when he reached Denver City. Then he thought of a whole week of relaxation. A whole week. Just as he was closing his eyes, he thought he saw the stars overhead twinkle gold.

Through the ground, Fargo felt footsteps moving through the potato field some distance away. Was it a dream? No, the footsteps were real. His mind leapt to attention. He eased his hand up toward the Colt lying on the bedroll beside his head. He opened his eyes to slits. The sky was pale blue, with the predawn light and the mockingbirds were noisy already. The footsteps did not falter but moved carefully with hardly a sound, heel placed gently, followed in a soft silent roll with the arch and then the toes. Only a light-footed Indian moved that gracefully, Fargo thought in a flash. An Indian on foot this close to the way station did not bode well. The steps were coming straight toward him and in a moment would be upon him. Fargo tensed and leapt to his feet, Colt before him.

Laurel's wide eyes met his and her face paled. She gasped and fell back a step as she saw Fargo jump up from underneath the cottonwood.

"It's okay," he said, immediately lowering his pistol. "I didn't mean to frighten you. You move as quietly as a Sioux tracking buffalo!"

"I'm sorry!" she said, blushing and looking toward the eastern horizon, away from his gaze and away from the sight of him in his underdrawers. "I wasn't expecting to run into anybody out here."

"What are you doing out so early? And alone?" Fargo asked, scooping up his clothes and pulling them on.

"I like this time of morning. I was curious to see what the land looked like," she said, keeping her eyes carefully averted as he dressed.

"It's not safe to be strolling around by yourself. This isn't Beacon Hill," he admonished her. "Anyway, where did you learn to creep around like that? At the Boston Girls' Boarding School?"

She laughed and chanced a glance at him. He had dressed and was buttoning his shirt.

"Actually, yes," Laurel said. "Every weekend, the teachers took us hiking out near Concord. Sometimes we even camped out. The school believed in rigorous training of all kinds—'strong bodies, strong minds,' they said."

Fargo noticed that she spoke easily, losing the shy hesitation from the day before.

"I loved hiking. I've read a lot about the outdoors. Especially books by James Fenimore Cooper. He explained how the Indians walked when hunting. I always thought about it when we hiked and I practiced to see how quietly I could walk."

"Very impressive," Fargo said. She was full of surprises, he thought. Fargo saw her gaze follow the splash of rising sun. She turned to look westward at the rosy snow-covered peaks.

"This is beautiful country," she said, and Fargo heard the passionate enthusiasm in her voice. And, as if she had showed him too much, she blushed again and turned away to hide her expression.

"I like it too," Fargo said quietly.

"You must, from the stories you told last night," Laurel said. "It was like the books had come to life for me. Like a dream come true. Did you really have all those adventures?" Any trace of diffidence was gone and her voice was strong and forthright.

"You haven't heard the half of it," Fargo said with a laugh.

"I hope I'll have a chance to hear more of your stories," she said.

"Anytime," Fargo agreed. In the distance, from the direction of the farmhouse, he heard a promising clatter of pots and pans. "But let's not hold up breakfast."

Fargo rolled up his bedroll and carried it with one hand, while he took her arm with the other and they headed toward the farmhouse. She moved beside him as lightly as the morning breeze, the rays of sun glittering in her loose blond hair. She was very young, he thought. Sixteen maybe. But independent and, he thought again, full of surprises.

The company had assembled and was digging into flapjacks when Skye slid into his seat next to Pru.

"Sleep well?" he asked her quietly with a wink and a smile.

"Didn't dream of tiddlywinks," she answered under her breath, and he felt her warm hand under the table slide quickly across his thigh.

After breakfast, Fargo went into the yard, followed by Sam and the driver. As they came out onto the front porch, they saw that Maximus Sweedler had tied the painted cart behind the mountain wagon and was now trying to hitch his two mules. They were not cooperating. The larger one had dug his heels in and was braying as Maximus tried to drag him toward the wagon.

"You godforsaken jackass!" he yelled at the mule. Maximus pulled a heavy ox whip from his belt and unwound it in a fury, raising it above his head and bringing it down with great force across the mule's back. He raised the whip high behind him for a second blow.

Fargo crossed the yard in a flash and just as the whip began to descend, he caught the leather strip in his fist. When the whip resisted, Maximum wheeled about in surprise.

"What the hell?" he screamed. "What do you think you're doing?"

"Whipping a mule doesn't help," Fargo said evenly, maintaining his firm grip on the leather thong as Maximus tries to wrench it from him. Sam had come up behind Fargo.

"He'll go if you give him something nice," Sam said.

Sam reached deep into his pants pocket and pulled out something Fargo couldn't see. Probably sugar, he thought. He watched as Sam held out his hand to the mule, who looked back at him suspiciously.

"Get out of my way," Maximus said impatiently, trying to elbow Fargo aside. Fargo stood firm, continuing to hold one end of the whip.

"Give it a minute," Skye said, watching Sam.

Maximus shrugged and backed away and Fargo released the whip. Sam held out his hand and spoke in a low voice and the mule's large ears came forward and its nose twitched. The mule took a hesitant step and touched its bristly muzzle to Sam's palm, and ate what it found there. Sam hooked a finger through the bridle and led the mule easily to a place between the traces of the mountain wagon.

"Still say I could've got him moving with the whip," Maximus grumbled while he hitched the mule and Sam led the other one forward.

"Can't stand to see anybody mistreat an animal," Fargo said as he and Sam retreated.

" 'Specially mules," Sam added. "They're such good critters. A mule will die for you if you handle 'em right. Why, take my old Bessie for example. God rest her mulish soul. Many's the time she saved my life on the trail," Sam said, shaking his head.

"All I can say is, I wouldn't want to be a mule and haul a load for that snake-oil salesman," Fargo added and moved off to take care of his horse.

The Ovaro had eaten well and looked fit, and was stamping impatiently, eager for the trail. Fargo curried the horse, admiring the sleek black-and-white coat and the rippling muscles in the powerful chest and legs. He checked the hooves, removing two small stones. The shoes were on firmly. Fargo saddled and bridled the horse, then strapped on his bedroll and saddle bags. He was as eager to ride out as his horse was.

Meanwhile, the driver, assisted by Sam, assembled the stagecoach team and loaded the bags into the rear boot. Fargo sauntered over to the porch where the coach passengers waited.

"Only seventeen miles to go to Denver City," he said to Pru. "You riding in the coach today or with me?"

"Bouncing Betty! I'm still sore from yesterday," she said with a wink. "I think I'll take the coach."

"Suit yourself," he said. "It's probably better. Today we'll be going through Arapaho territory. I'll be out front, scouting."

"Will we see Indians today?" Laurel asked, overhearing his remark. Fargo could tell from her tone of voice that she was looking forward to her first glimpse of Indians.

"They steer clear of stagecoach trails," Fargo answered. "They'll see us, but we won't see them. Unless they want us to."

"Will they attack?" Pru asked, sudden fear in her voice.

"The tribe has been under treaty and has been peaceful in these parts," Fargo said. "But, you never know what might set them off again and it's better to keep a keen eye out."

"One more reason I'm glad you happened on to us," Cavendish put in, as he helped the ladies into the coach and got inside himself, shutting the door.

"Are you, perchance, heading for Denver City?" Maximus Sweedler's high voice cut in. He was sitting atop the mountain wagon with his wife beside him. Fargo knew Maximus had heard every word about their destination and the Arapaho. The courteous thing would be to suggest that the Sweedlers follow the stagecoach.

35

"Yup," Fargo answered. He was not feeling courteous. Let Sweedler ask, he thought as he swung up onto his horse.

"M-m-mind if we follow along?"

Sweedler only seemed to stutter when unsure of himself.

"Plenty of room for anybody on the trail," Fargo said noncommittally. The two mules, which moved more slowly than the coach, would hold them back by maybe an hour's travel time. Fargo would have to set a slower pace in order that the Sweedlers wouldn't fall too far behind. Of course, he thought, if there was trouble on the way to Denver City, he would help the Sweedlers. But he didn't like them—not the fat, pompous, cheating salesman, nor his pointy-faced, quiet wife.

The short wagon train creaked and jolted forward, moving out of the stable yard. The Trailsman led, tall and lean on the magnificent Ovaro, followed by the six-horse team pulling the Concord coach, the two mules hauling the Sweedler's low mountain wagon, and their brightly painted cart.

The trail led over the gentle swells, avoiding the occasional rocky ravines which sliced open the plains. The morning sun slanted across the bluegrass and turned the distant snow-covered peaks bright white.

After an hour's ride, Fargo sighted the dip in the plains which indicated the beginning of Cherry Creek. The trail swung westward and followed the creek downstream into Denver City. Ahead was a nice place to stop for clear, fresh water. Unfortunately, it was too early in the season for the luscious wild cherries which lined the banks.

Just then, he saw a cloud of dust over the horizon to the west, a subtle yellow smudge rising against the hills. Fargo spurred the Ovaro and wheeled about toward the coach.

"Pull up for a few minutes," he said to the driver and Sam, keeping his voice low so the passengers wouldn't hear. "Keep the Sweedlers near you too and a sharp eye out. I think there are Indians over the next rise. And, from the look of that cloud of dust, there are a helluva lot of them on the move. It could be a war party."

Fargo turned his horse to the west and rode toward the

36

rise, scanning the sharp horizon, which remained empty. If the Arapaho were on the warpath, the scouts would fan out far ahead and to the sides of the advancing party. He should see the scouts already on the horizon, but they weren't there. What was going on?

Fargo slowed the horse as he came to the top of the rise and then moved forward by inches until his vision just cleared the valley below. The Arapaho camp—the entire tribe, it looked to Fargo—was on the move. Ponies, women, children, and even the dogs were loaded with packs and were dragging travois and rolled-up tepees. There were hundreds of Indians, strung out in a wide V, moving across the valley. Despite the appearance of chaos—the barking of the dogs, the running children—the migration was a model of efficiency. Each pack was sized according to the strength of the bearer—small packs for the children and the eldery, and larger ones for the strong young women and muscular dogs—so that none would fall behind and slow the pace. The wide V-formation ensured that few of the Indians walked in each other's dust.

The braves rode in a large protective circle ahead and to the sides. Fargo could see a string of them climbing the slope on the opposite side of the valley. The scouts would be ascending the slope in front of Fargo, he knew, and would come into his sight at any moment.

Fargo knew the Arapaho had a large camp by the Platte River in recent years, a few miles out of Denver City. This time of year they should be settled in, he thought, sending out small parties to hunt the summer buffalo.

Fargo wondered if he should risk trying to find out what was going on. A large migration like this smelled of some kind of trouble. Were the Arapaho being driven away by the settlers? If so, they wouldn't be in any mood for a friendly powwow. The Trailsman narrowed his eyes and scanned the scouting braves on the opposite slope of the valley. No war paint. No shields or ritual battle headdresses.

A confrontation might be worth the risk, the Trailsman decided, and he moved the Ovaro forward to stand on the top of the crest so his tall figure would be silhouetted against the bright sky. Immediately, he saw the side scouts ascending the hill below him and they spotted Fargo too. Three of them broke off to ride in his direction. They didn't hurry, Fargo saw, which was a good sign and he didn't move, a signal to them that he wished to talk.

As they came near, one of them rode forward, one hung back a respectful distance, and the other galloped over the crest behind Fargo, to be sure that Fargo was not bait for an ambush.

The brave who approached the Trailsman was bronze muscled and proud. His long hair whipped behind him in the wind and the sun glinted on the single iridescent blue feather he wore at the crown of his head. Fargo's quarter-Indian blood made him appreciate the gracefulness of the brave riding bareback on his chestnut-and-white dappled pinto, the horse and the rider moving as one. Fargo held up his right hand in the greeting sign as the brave halted, twenty feet away.

"Good weather for travel," Fargo said in Algonquian. He had picked up enough basic vocabulary to make himself understood. He hoped. The Indian grunted agreement, his dark eyes watching the Trailsman carefully.

"In summer, the Arapaho stay by the Platte. Hunt buffalo. Dry meat. Wait for cherries to make pemmican for winter." Fargo said, hoping his Algonquian was comprehensible. "Why do you leave this place?"

The brave sat immobile. "Bad winter," he said.

'Bad winter' meaning no food? Fargo thought. Perhaps the tribe was hungry. But this brave looked well fed. 'Bad winter' meaning trouble with the Denver City settlers? But there was no war paint, no threat.

"Bad winter," the brave said again. "Much snow."

This was getting nowhere, Fargo thought. "When will you return?" he asked.

"We come back when mountains are green," the Indian replied and sat looking at Fargo without expression for a long time, as if his words had explained everything. Fargo felt there was nothing more to be learned.

"May buffalo run to your arrows," he said to the brave.

The Indian nodded, a flash of surprise on his face that a white man knew this ancient farewell.

"And your arrows find the hearts of your enemies," the Indian replied. When he wheeled on the pinto and galloped back down the slope, the other two following.

Fargo was lost in thought as he rode back toward the waiting coach and the wagon. He mulled over the brave's words. Bad winter. It was possible the Indians were withdrawing in order to muster an attack on settlers, or on Denver City itself. Fargo played with that possibility. His instinct told him it wasn't right. He galloped up to the stagecoach. Paul Cavendish stood outside, his hand on his ivory-grip Sharp pistol.

"No problem," Fargo said. "The Arapaho tribe's on the move. Damn if I can figure why. But, we're not in danger. Let's move out."

As they rode the last two hours into Denver City, the brave's words echoed in Fargo's ears: "May your arrows find the hearts of your enemies."

Fargo led the train down from the top of the rolling hills and along Cherry Creek, down the gentle slope into the wide bowl. At the bottom of the valley, two rivers met—the Platte and Cherry Creek. There, on the sandy and rocky banks, sprouted Denver City.

A mile outside of town, Fargo's sharp hearing picked up the noises of the city—the horses whinnying, a smithy's hammer on iron, wagons creaking under their loads, shouting voices, dogs barking, and the sound of furious sawing and hammering. They passed the cemetery, a hill surrounded by an iron fence, with its wooden markers askew.

Then they rode between clapboard houses, which became closer and closer. Then came stores, warehouses, stables, and saloons. The dusty streets were suddenly crowded with rigs and wagons and mules and horses, the boardwalks full of swaggering men and colorfully dressed ladies.

At high noon, they reached the stagecoach office. Fargo pulled up outside, dismounted and tethered the Ovaro. The coach passengers dismounted, rubbing their muscles which ached from the long hours in the coach.

"See you around," Maximus Sweedler called out, as he guided his lumbering wagon past them, looking, no doubt, for a crowded corner from which to hawk his wares.

Fargo sauntered over to Pru, who stood looking all around her in amazement.

"Holy hellhole!" she exclaimed. "This is Denver City? This collection of shanties and dirt?" She shuddered as she looked down the street clogged with carriages and rising dust. She raised her parasol and balanced it on her shoulder.

"Yup, this is the big city," Fargo said, laughing. "Don't worry. It kinda grows on you."

"I think it's just beautiful," Laurel said, looking around, her pale blue eyes wide with excitement. Pru rolled her eyes and turned away from them.

"Don't go overboard," Cavendish admonished his daughter. "Denver City's got potential. Someday it will be a real city, but it's still pretty raw as yet." He patted Laurel on the shoulder and she smiled up at him.

"Fargo, I'm putting you up at Fanny's for the week," Cavendish said. He pointed to a large square three-story building with FANNY'S written in large letters on a signboard across the front. "Best place in town. Tell Fanny I sent you and tell her to give you a room at the top. Then the late night fist fights won't disturb your rest. Right now, I need to get Laurel home. Meet me at the mint in about an hour's time. It's over that way, but anyone on the street can give you directions."

"I'll be there," Fargo said. Cavendish gave instructions for the bags to be sent around to the house and escorted Laurel down the boardwalk. Laurel turned to wave goodbye to Fargo, her excitement showing in the two bright pink spots on her cheeks.

Pru still stood looking out over the city's bustle. Then she wheeled around. "So, what's the deal with you and Cavendish?" Pru asked. She kept her voice light and disinterested, and twirled her parasol idly. But, Fargo heard the sharp edge of something that was more than just curiosity.

"Why do you want to know?" he said nonchalantly. "Can't a man have some private business? What's your interest in the mint anyway? I noticed it last night."

"Are you cooking up some conspiracy with Cavendish?" she asked, her voice firmer.

"I can't say," Fargo said simply and quietly, wanting her to drop the matter.

"Why not?"

"Look, Pru," Fargo said. "Just drop it. I'll tell you when I can."

He saw her brown eyes blaze with sudden anger and something like pain crossed her face.

"Private business," she spat, anger sharpening every consonant. She turned away from him.

"Whoa!" Fargo said. "What happened to the Tiddlywink Princess of last night?"

"I didn't know you were involved in the mint too," Pru said, refusing to look him in the face.

"I might be and I might not be," Fargo said. "But what difference does it make to you?" He grasped her shoulders and turned her around, pulling her toward him forcefully. She resisted, but he wrapped one strong arm around her softness and lifted her face upward to look into her eyes.

He brushed her lips with his, then said quietly, "Now, Pru. What's going on here? What do you know about the mint? Or Cavendish?"

"You're already in cahoots with him!" Pru said, pulling back. "I can see that, I'm no fool. Tramlin' turncoats! I didn't think you'd end up being one of them."

"One of who, Pru?" Fargo asked.

"You just don't see it, do you?" Pru said, pushing him away and shaking her head. "Things aren't always what they seem. I learned that a long time ago."

Pru stumbled down the steps and Fargo saw her wipe tears from her eyes. She headed toward Fanny's.

"See you around," he called after her. She pretended not to hear him.

Women are strange creatures, Fargo thought, watching her energetic and round figure weaving among the pedestrians on the boardwalk. He would have to get to the bottom of this and find out what Pru knew about the mint and about Cavendish. Meanwhile, Fargo would keep his eyes and ears open. Things certainly were not what they seemed.

Fargo looked around for Sweeteye Sam, but he had disappeared. He untied the Ovaro and led him down the street to the stables. Walking ahead of him were three young girls, who giggled when they saw him eyeing them appreciatively. There were a lot of beautiful women in Denver City. It was going to be a helluva week.

"Gorgeous, ain't she?" Sam asked. "Look at those ankles and that long neck. Not to mention that magnificent chest. God, that's beautiful."

"I don't know," Fargo said doubtfully.

"What do you mean you don't know?" Sam asked. "She's the most gorgeous creature I ever laid eyes on. Look at that round rear . . . the way the muscles ripple every time she moves. Just does something to me. And those eyes—clear as a winter night and brown as chestnuts. I have to have her."

"So? Why don't you?" Fargo asked.

"Price is too high," Sam answered.

"You can afford it," Fargo said. "You just told me you've got seven pokes full of nuggets and gold dust. Live a little. If you want her, just have her."

"I dunno," Sam said. "Hey you! How about forty dollars?" he called out to a man in a red shirt, sitting in the corner.

"Not enough," the man said. "It's eighty-five."

Sam turned back to contemplate his beauty.

"Seems alright for a healthy mule," Fargo said. "Come on, Sam. Enjoy yourself."

"I'll think about it," Sam said, digging in his pocket and holding his hand out toward the mule in the pen. It ambled slowly over, extended its long pink tongue and licked Sam's palm, then nuzzled it. He stroked its long nose and scratched its ears. "You beautiful ass. You act like Bessie and you look like Bessie too," he murmured to the mule. "Bessietoo! You like that name don't you?"

Fargo left Sam where he had found him in the stable yard, hanging over the fence and blissfully muttering to the mule. He walked over toward the man in the red shirt sitting in the corner of the shady porch, whittling in the shade.

"I need to stable my Ovaro for a week," Fargo said. "The best oats and a daily curry."

"This is the finest stable in town," the man said. "Ask anyone."

"I'll do that," Fargo said with a smile, putting down the deposit. "I need a receipt."

"Sure," he said. But before the man had a chance to pick up the coins, a voice cut in.

"I need my horse and I need it now." The words were spit out forcefully and malevolently.

"Just a minute, Mr. Booth," the stable owner answered, scooping up the coins and fumbling in his shirt pocket for his receipt book.

"I don't have time to wait," Booth's voice said again. Fargo turned very slowly on his heels and looked the man up and down.

Booth was tall, with wavy brown hair and large brown eyes. His body was powerful and graceful. But his eyes and cheeks were sunken, and Fargo could sense his restlessness, as if he were haunted by ghosts or demons.

"What're you looking at?" he said to Fargo. The stable-owner was still fumbling with the receipt book. "Get my horse now," Booth said. "You can do that after."

"I believe I was here first," Fargo said quietly.

"Wanna make something of it?" Booth said threateningly, unsnapping the pistol strap on his holster. The Trailsman touched his Colt with the tips of his fingers, keeping his eye on Booth. The man was on an incredibly short fuse, he thought.

Booth backed away a few steps, moving past Sam, as if he was ready to draw. Sam was watching carefully. The stabler shrank back in the corner, out of the range of fire, nervously scribbling in his receipt book.

"Hardly seems worth it," Fargo said with a smile.

"No, I guess you're right. You don't seem worth it," Booth taunted. Then he dropped his hand away from his pistol. Fargo shrugged, ignoring the insult. He turned toward the owner to take the receipt and behind him he heard the unmistakable whisper of Booth's pistol coming out of the holster.

Fargo shoved the owner out of the line of fire and dove to the ground, rolled twice and came up on his feet, drawing his Colt at the same moment. But it wasn't necessary.

"You goddamn dust digger!" Booth yelled, rubbing his eyes with one hand. The pistol dangled uselessly in his other hand and Sam stood beside Booth, ready to throw another fistful of dirt in his face.

In an instant, Fargo had crossed the yard and taken the pistol from Booth's grip, emptied it of cartridges and threw it down in front of him. Hatred blazed in Booth's watery eyes.

"If you're looking for trouble, Mister," Fargo said to Booth. "Don't come looking in my direction. Come on, Sam." Fargo picked up the receipt from the man in the red shirt. They walked out onto the bustling street.

"Thanks for the help," Fargo said.

"Nothing to it," Sam said. "What do you suppose was eating him?"

"Got me," Fargo said. "Booth won't live long if he's running around being that touchy. By the way, Sam, you're a useful man to have around in a fight."

"Anytime I can be of service," Sam said. "Right now, I'm heading over to the mint to get my dust weighed in. These seven pokes are burning a hole in my backside."

"I'm heading toward the mint too," Fargo said.

"How about a little liquid refreshment first?" Sam asked, eyeing a saloon. "I'll buy."

They walked through the swinging doors into the saloon. A few solitary men sat drinking and a quiet card game was in progress in the back.

Fargo and Sam stood at the bar.

"Taos lightning," Sam said. "And one for my friend."

As the bartender brought the bottle and the glasses, Sam lifted up his buckskin jacket to reveal the seven pokes, also made of buckskin, tied to his belt. He untied one of them and put it on the counter.

"I fill the pokes with gold. Comes in three sizes, you know—nuggets, shot and gold dust. Then I soak 'em in the stream and put 'em on a rock to dry in the sun," he explained to Fargo. "Pretty soon, the buckskin shrinks around the gold dust and holds it real tight and compact. Keeps it from shifting and coming out the seams and the top."

"How much?" he asked the fat bartender.

"Two bits for a shot of Taos lightning," the man answered. "One pinch a quarter, just like everywhere else."

Sam opened the drawstring on the top of the poke and held it open toward the bartender. The fat man took a pinch of the gold, reaching deep into the bag with his fat fingers. He carefully dropped the pinch of gold shot into a bowl behind him on the bar, and turned back to Sam's poke for a second pinch to pay for Fargo's drink.

"You sure got long fingernails," Sam complained as the bartender's fingers came up with the second pinch.

"Just like every other bartender in town," the man said, without smiling.

"Ain't that the truth," Sam said. "Gold dust is a mess to spend and to keep. I learned pretty fast to trade it in as soon as I hit town, for a whole lot of reasons."

"I just saw one," Fargo said, nodding toward the bartender.

"Course, it goes both ways," Sam said. "Some fellas fill their pokes with brass filings. And they manage to get out of town before it's discovered. In any case, the mint is a godsend for us prospectors, since it collects the stuff, melts it down, and you know exactly what you've got."

"Let's get on to the mint," Fargo said. "Bottoms up."

Taos lightning cuts a jagged line through your insides. Fargo suspected that's how it got its name and he could still feel its path when they got to the mint.

The two-story brick building was distinguished by tall narrow front windows and a large sign which read AURARIA PRIVATE MINT AND BANK. A stream of people were entering and exiting the double-width front doors.

Fargo and Sam went inside. The large airy front room was arranged like an ordinary bank. The four tellers, wearing eyeshades and sleeve garters, stood in a barred cage behind a waist high countertop. Behind them, a large man stood guard. Sam and Fargo joined the line of customers and were soon at a window.

The teller pushed four shallow metal dishes under the bars toward Sam, who lined up the seven gold pokes on the countertop. He carefully poured the contents of each of the bags onto the dishes and pushed them under the bars, watching carefully as the teller weighed them.

"Forty-nine ounces," the teller said, after weighing each

of the dishes and tallying them up. "Pretty good trip you had. Right now, the rate's sixteen dollars an ounce. That makes seven hundred and eighty-four dollars and fifty-five cents."

"That's a lot of mules," Fargo said, as the teller counted out the gold eagles. Sam spread his bandana out on the counter and piled the gleaming gold coins in the middle. Then he tied the ends and shoved the heavy bundle into one of his big front pockets, where it made an obvious bulge. He pulled the flap down over the pocket and tied it shut with the buckskin thongs sewn on for that purpose.

"Could you tell Mr. Cavendish that Skye Fargo is here to see him?" Fargo asked the teller. The clerk whispered to the large man who emerged from the cage and rapped on a wide door off to the side.

In a moment, Fargo saw Cavendish appear at the door. "Don't tell me you waited in line?" he said to Fargo. "Come on in."

"Mind if Sam joins us?" Fargo asked. "He's a good man to have along in a tight situation."

"You haven't told me what you're up to. But I can sure guess well enough," Sam said quietly.

Cavendish paused a moment and looked the old prospector up and down.

"Hm," Cavendish said. "Prospecting! Might be just the thing!" He opened the door wide. "Come on in, Sam. Fargo."

They entered Cavendish's office, a large imposing room with no windows, flanked by wooden file cabinets. Behind Cavendish's oak desk was the door of a large safe built solidly into the wall.

"Let me guess," Sam said, as he settled himself comfortably into one of the leather chairs. "You're trying to get a gold shipment out of Denver City. Let's say a big shipment."

"Accurate," Cavendish said.

"Course it's accurate. Everybody in town's talking about it. I heard about it from the stable owner when I asked 'What's new?' So, you're hiring the Trailsman here to find a new trail."

"Could be. What else did you hear from the stable owner?" Cavendish asked.

"I heard you got together a team of men to guard the gold on the way back east, a dozen of them, all sharpshooters, all old hands at gold shipping, led by some young whipper-snapper named Wyatt Roundtree. I heard you're even throwing 'em a farewell party next Saturday night."

"You heard a lot," Fargo said.

"I told you this is a talking town," Cavendish said to Fargo.

"Sure is," Fargo agreed. "Sounds like you've got the shipment all planned and all I have to do is guide."

"Actually, I've thought of another plan for you, Fargo. And it involves Sam," Cavendish said, unrolling a map of Colorado Territory on the desk in front of him. "Have to keep everybody in town guessing, you see. Rather than send you off with the gold shipment, I'd like to stake the two of you to a little mining expedition." Paul stared down at the map in front of him and his finger moved in a large circle around Denver City, a slow smile spreading on his face.

3

"Prospecting?" Fargo asked. "Not my line of work."

"You'll only look like you're prospecting," Cavendish assured him. "We'll load up a wagon with pick axes and saws, pans, provisions. But underneath the equipment, across the bottom of the wagon, you'll carry the gold ingots."

"What about Wyatt Roundtree and his men?" Sam asked.

"They're the decoy," Fargo guessed.

"Exactly," said Cavendish. "My plan is to send off Wyatt and his team with a good-bye party at Fanny's, the likes of which this town has never seen. All the hubbub is sure to attract the conspirators. They'll follow the decoy team and a couple of days later, you'll depart quietly on a prospecting expedition."

"Which trail will the decoy team take?" Fargo asked thoughtfully, stroking his strong jaw with one hand.

"I'm sending them out on the Smoky Hill route," Cavendish answered. "That would be the safest way for a real gold shipment and would be what the bandits would expect."

"You have a route for us in mind already?" Fargo asked.

"Nope. I thought I'd leave that up to you, what with your mighty reputation as the Trailsman."

"Where would you go with a load of new mining equipment, Sam?" Fargo asked the grizzled old prospector.

Sam's eyes brightened with a faraway look.

"They say Pike's Peak is bust, but I don't agree. I think there's some glitter left in those hills."

"Pike's Peak then," Fargo said. "At least we'll head southward for the first few days. Then we'll blaze a new trail, striking out east."

"Will it work?" Cavendish asked.

"Might," Fargo said.

"Take this money and start buying equipment tomorrow," Cavendish said, tossing a heavy bag of coins across the desk. "The word will get around that you're outfitting for a prospecting venture. It would look suspicious if people knew I staked you. So, the story is you and Sam have pooled your money."

"And what about old Sam?" Sam asked impatiently. "I gather you need somebody who knows prospecting to make this whole ruse work. You need Sweeteye Sam, you do. You going to make me an offer?"

"Eight hundred dollars and you can keep the equipment," Cavendish offered.

"A thousand," Sam replied, a light in his eyes.

"Eight hundred seventy," Cavendish said, trying to sound reluctant. "Not a penny more."

"Nine fifty and you're on," Sam replied.

"You got it," Cavendish replied, extending his hand to Sam and then to Fargo. "Let's have a drink and a fine dinner to bind the deal. Fanny's Saloon has the best grub in town, bar none."

"Surely big strong boys like you eat just one more steak?" Fanny said encouragingly as she placed a platter piled high with rare steaks on the table in front of them.

Fargo, Sam, and Cavendish had eaten well. And then they had consumed some more. And then, because Fanny insisted, they had had just one more helping, very slowly. Now the three men were leaning dangerously back in their chairs, having eaten much too much. Cavendish had just lit a cigar and was offering one to Fargo and Sam, when Fanny arrived with yet one more plate of steaks.

"Honey, there's hardly room in here to take a breath, much less put another steak inside," Cavendish protested, patting his belly.

Fanny pouted, placed her hands on the table in front of her and eyed the three of them, her plump breasts nearly popping out of her tight bodice and her round full figure straining a colorful plaid dress.

"Well, Paul," she said with a trace of impatience, after a moment of silence when it became apparent that none of the three could be persuaded to eat a fourth helping, "how come you came in here if you didn't want to eat?"

"Must be the scenery," Cavendish said. Fargo saw him give Fanny a discreet pinch. It was clear that the grub was not the only attraction at Fanny's Saloon, at least for Paul Cavendish.

Fargo leaned back to savor the Havana cigar, inhaling the rich sweet smoke slowly, relaxed and lost in thought. He half closed his eyes and slowly surveyed the bustling room.

At the tables were cowhands, ranchers, city folks, and gambling men, all eating or fending off Fanny's waitresses who brought more plates of food. At one end of the long room, a wide stairway led upstairs to the rooms for rent, where Fargo's gear had been stowed. A hot bath and a nap were what he needed, Fargo thought.

When on vacation, indulge, he told himself.

He wondered vaguely what time it was and his eyes went to the imposing grandfather clock on the stair landing. Above the clock was a sign on the wall which read CLOSING TIME: MIDNIGHT BY THIS CLOCK. STRICTLY ENFORCED. The face read one thirty, but it was certainly three or four o'clock, Fargo reasoned. He noted that the brass disc on the clock's pendulum hung motionless.

Just then, he heard the doors swing open and a familiar voice grated on his nerves.

"You would certainly benefit from this miraculous Kickapoo Oil," the high quavering voice said, unmistakably that of Maximus Sweedler's.

"Excellent for man or beast," Sweedler continued and Fargo saw a well-dressed gentleman push through the swinging doors into the saloon, followed closely by Sweedler. The gentleman hurried toward the bar in a vain effort to shake the pesky snake-oil salesman.

"This Kickapoo oil cures the toothache, headache, sore throat, chillblains, frostbite, neuralgia, and rheumatic pains of any description. Only thirty cents for a handy bottle of health!"

Sweedler took a breath.

"No. My final no," the man said quickly. "Leave me alone once and for all."

The man turned back to the bar. Sweedler's sharp eyes swept the room and came to rest on Fargo, Cavendish, and Sam.

"Oh, my friends!" he said advancing on them. "Do let me thank you again Mr. Fargo for the accompaniment into this fair city through the dangerous territory beyond! Allow me to shake your hand in eternal gratitude. If there is ever anything I can do for you, such as providing any kind of ointment or medicinal—at a bargain price available only to my dear friends—then, of course I will render this service. Are any of you three gentlemen at the present moment experiencing any kind of physical discomfort of any description?"

"I was just fine until about one minute ago," Fargo muttered.

"And what are your symptoms? Sudden fever? Chills? Dizziness perhaps? These things are going around right now," Sweedler said, shaking his head.

"Something, or someone, is giving me a severe case of indigestion," Fargo said.

Sam guffawed and Cavendish smiled.

"The dyspepsia! The scourge of civilized man! And womankind," he added, tipping his hat to Fanny who stood beside Cavendish, giggling behind her plump upraised hand.

"Only one thing to do! A strong dose of Doctor Yellowart's Intestinal Carbonate! That will do the trick."

Sweedler paused and fished about in his vest pockets, drawing out one long thin glass bottle after another.

"No, I do not seem to have Dr. Yellowart's Elixer on me. Wilhelmina!" he called out suddenly. "Wilhelmina!"

Fargo saw the batwing doors part slowly and the auburn-haired, quiet woman entered awkwardly, her hands clasping the bars of the painted cart, which she pulled with some effort inside the saloon after her. There was a stunned silence at all of the tables and everyone turned to watch.

As soon as the back of the cart had cleared the door by several feet, Wilhelmina loosened a crossbar with one foot which swung down to the floor and held the cart in place.

Then she quickly moved to the side of the cart and opened one flap to display the familiar circus lettering.

"My friends," Sweedler began in a loud voice, backing up toward the cart and gesturing grandly toward the open flap and the rows of bottles within. "You are about to be blessed. Blessed with the opportunity, I say the opportunity, for eternal good health, robust physique, and the banishment—yes, I say the banishment—of all of mankind's ills and plagues! Let me begin by curing this poor man's excruciating indigestion. My dear," he said to Mrs. Sweedler, "please fetch a dose of the good Doctor Yellowart's Carbonate."

Wilhelmina began to search for the bottle among the rows of others and Fargo heard Fanny come to life behind them.

"Wait just a cotton picking minute!" she called out, her plump figure moving quickly through the tables and chairs toward the cart. "Just what do you think you are doing?"

"Ah, madam," Maximus said, accenting the second syllable and bowing low, sweeping his hand in a large circle toward the floor. "You must be the proprietress of this fine establishment."

"I own this joint if that's what you mean," Fanny said in a no-nonsense voice.

"Let me explain that I am only fulfilling a request for a digestive aid from one of your patrons, Mr. Fargo."

"I didn't hear Skye Fargo request any such thing," Fanny retorted. "Did you want some of this snake oil, Skye?" she asked.

"Never said I did," Skye answered.

"But he was suffering from acute indigestion," Sweedler protested. "Surely you would not want one of your patrons to suffer needlessly, when there is a cure available."

"Did you get a stomachache from my grub?" Fanny asked Skye.

"Fanny, I was happily digesting away," Skye explained, "when all of a sudden I heard this jabbering voice and my stomach just tightened right up!"

The crowd in the saloon laughed.

"That's just what I thought you meant," Fanny said. "That's it, Mr. Maximus-What's-Your-Name. You get this

52

circus out of my saloon. I run a quiet place here where people can digest in peace!"

The two deputies at the bar took a step forward and Sweedler quickly backed toward the cart, lowered the flap and pushed it through the swinging doors with Wilhelmina's assistance.

"If that ain't the damndest thing!" Fanny said when she returned to Fargo's table. "Imagine bringing that wagon inside my saloon and trying to hawk that stuff right here under my own nose!"

"You sure did drive them off, ma'am," Sam said, admiringly.

"Here's a toast to a force of nature—Fanny!" Fargo proposed, raising his nearly empty glass.

"Fanny!" Cavendish and Sam echoed.

Fanny blushed and looked pleased. "Well, I'd better be getting the cook to work on dinner. What time is it?" she asked, looking at the grandfather clock. "Oh! It's stopped!"

"Probably just needs winding," Fargo suggested.

"No, I wound it myself this morning. I'm afraid it's broken. That's bad luck for me. I depend on that clock at closing time. Otherwise, everybody's pocket watch says there's another ten minutes to closing time and I can't get the fellas out of here. This is serious, boys."

"There must be a clock maker in town who can fix it," Cavendish said.

"There is," Fanny said, "But he's gone to Cheyenne and won't be back for a month. Meanwhile, I'm going to have four weeks of chaos every evening at closing time."

"Mrs. Sweedler!" Cavendish said, thumping the table. "She fixed my pocket watch in a flash the night before we reached Denver City."

"That skinny woman with the salesman? I can't ask her. I just threw her out of my saloon," Fanny protested. She was silent for a moment looking at the grandfather clock and considering. "Still, it's going to be a lot of trouble around here without that clock."

"I'll see if I can talk her into it," Fargo volunteered.

Fargo exited the saloon and quickly spotted the Sweedlers,

setting up shop just down the street. He walked toward them rapidly as they were opening the flap of the cart.

"Excuse me, but . . ." he began.

"Knew you'd be back for the carbonate elixir," Sweedler said, wheeling at the sound of his voice. "Wise man. No need to suffer without cause when there's a remedy at hand . . ."

"It's about Mrs. Sweedler," Fargo interrupted and saw the surprise on her husband's face. She came forward quietly, her dark eyes darting from Fargo's face to her husband's.

"It's the clock in the saloon," Fargo explained. "It seems to have stopped. I would like to pay you to fix it."

"Of course," she murmured, and followed Fargo into the saloon.

Wilhelmina Sweedler seemed to take on a kind of authority as she called for an oil lamp to be brought and held up so that she would be able to work inside the clock. Fanny handed her the key to the glass door and she opened it, then unfastened the face and swung it forward to reveal the cogs and innerworkings.

"A simple matter," she said confidently and Fargo heard the slight foreign accent in her pronunciation. Once again he watched as she removed the flat box from her skirt pocket and her long fingers manipulated the delicate tools to adjust the clock mechanism.

After a moment, she was finished. She stepped down and gently pushed the pendulum to one side and released it. It swung to the other side and then returned. The slow steady ticking of the grandfather clock resumed.

"Five dollars?" Fargo asked.

Wilhelmina nodded and extended her long white hand toward him as he counted out the coins. When he had finished, he saw how tightly she closed her fingers around the golden coins.

"Why are you paying for my clock?" Fanny asked when she saw what Fargo was doing.

"Repaying you for curing my indigestion," Fargo answered.

Mrs. Sweedler neither acknowledged the payment, nor did she react to Fargo's words. She slipped out the front door of the saloon like a shadow.

Cavendish was preparing to return to the mint and Sam to the stable to visit Bessietoo. Fargo had his heart set on a hot bath and a nice long nap. Only one thing more would make it a perfect afternoon . . .

"Gallopin' goblins!" he heard, and he smiled with anticipation as he turned to watch the doorway. Pru's yellow parasol and shiny brown curls appeared over the top of the swinging doors which opened to admit her. She was happily chattering and batting her brown eyes as she lowered her parasol. She was not alone.

Beside Pru stood the tall unpleasant man from the stables. He bent down toward Pru, listening intently but hardly smiling.

Fargo heard Sam let out a low whistle.

"Mr. Trouble just walked through the door," Sam said under his breath.

"So I saw," Fargo answered quietly. He mentally checked the double-edged throwing knife in his calf holster and the position of his Colt. He quietly moved his hand down to the butt of the pistol and then released it.

"You two know that man?" Cavendish asked, sudden suspicion flaring up in his words.

"We had a run in with him at the stables this morning," Fargo explained. He saw Cavendish relax slightly at his answer.

"He's downright touchy!" Sam added.

What was Pru doing with such an unsavory character as Booth? Fargo wondered silently.

"What's his story?" said Skye.

"Matthew Booth was the director of the mint I told you about," said Paul. He explained to Sam, "Got caught skimming gold, or at least half the town thought he was guilty of it. The other half thought he was innocent. When he went to trial they had a hung jury. Twice. The case just tore the town in two."

"Sounds like Booth is either the slipperiest crook around or he's the unluckiest good guy," Fargo commented. "Though from our experience with him this afternoon, I tend to believe the worst of him."

"I just stay out of his way," Cavendish commented. "Innocent or guilty, Booth doesn't bear me any goodwill for replacing him. I'm slipping out the back. I'll see you around."

"I'll slip out with you," Sam said and they moved off together.

Fargo quietly moved to a corner table behind a noisy group of cowpokes. He lowered his hat over his eyes and leaned back against the wall to watch Pru and Booth.

They sat with their backs to him at a table toward the front of the saloon and ordered a meal. Booth inclined his head toward Pru and was listening intently. Fargo saw her reach over and take his hand beneath the table and then pat his cheek.

For a moment, Fargo toyed with the idea of approaching the table, calling Pru aside and asking her if she knew what she was doing with a man like Booth. But he quickly dismissed the fantasy. Pru was a big girl. She could make her own mistakes without him trying to save her from them.

There was no accounting for women's tastes, Fargo decided with a shrug. He rose quietly and stole up the stairs.

Sam longingly buffed the worked silver. The hollow cow horn had been fitted at the top and bottom with the intricately decorated metal, with one end shaped to be blown into. He lifted the smaller end and placed it to his lips. Fargo heard a sputter, then a low, haunting call filled the store, causing several of the other customers to wheel around.

"Might come in real handy, Skye," Sam said. "What if I'm panning one day over the ridge from you and I strike the mother lode? I could blow on this here thing and you would be there in a flash."

"Sam, we've got to have some money left over for the dynamite," Fargo said, eyeing the huge mountain of supplies piled on the middle of the shop's floor. He didn't want to give in too easily. He and Sam had to play the part of prospectors preparing for a long journey.

"Wouldn't take up much room either," Sam said, persisting. He blew on the horn again. It lowed mournfully like a lost steer. It was the kind of pure sound that could be heard for miles.

"How much is it, anyway?" Fargo asked, injecting a note of impatience into his voice.

"Twenty-five," Benny Wright said. Benny, a rotund man with striped suspenders, was the proprietor of the Denver Dry Goods Store, the largest supply store in town.

"Well, if you want that piece of cow horn, buy it yourself," said Fargo. They had to make this act realistic. "Tally up everything else and we'll load." Sam talked Benny down to eighteen dollars and fished the coins out of the personal stash in his pocket.

The pile of purchases included raw buckskin bags of varying sizes, braided rawhide and sisal rope, buckets for hauling the streambed gravel, pig-iron parts for constructing a sluice, an anvil, bellows and hammer, several flat metal gold-mining pans, pickaxes, shovels, a length of stout canvas, sledgehammers for breaking up the stones, extra pistols and rifles, round boxes of caps, casks of powder, bullets, and a wooden bucket for collecting bear grease, which Sam had said was essential.

Fargo and Sam had also selected barrels of flour and cornmeal, as well as bags of sugar, potatoes, beans, and coffee. Sam had picked out a new pair of boots, a buckskin jacket, and an oilskin slicker for use in downpours.

Benny totaled the purchases carefully and Fargo counted out the golden coins onto the wooden countertop.

"You sure are well-prepared," Benny said.

"You never know what you're going to find around Pike's Peak. There's some wild country up there."

"And it can get pretty wild around the mint at Philadelphia, too," Benny commented in a low, conspiratorial voice. Fargo shot a sharp look at the shopkeeper who glanced up at him and winked. What was Benny driving at? Did he suspect their real mission? Fargo kept his face blank and his voice innocent.

"Never been to Philadelphia," Fargo said, "so I'll have to take your word for that."

"Any destination can be pretty dangerous when you've got a load of gold," Benny said, looking Fargo straight in the eye.

"I'll keep that in mind if we hit a lucky strike," Skye answered noncommitally.

"I won't tell anyone though," Benny said suddenly, turning away and unlocking his cash drawer to deposit the coins. "Your secret is safe with me."

Fargo bid a hasty good-bye and retreated to the street where the loading had just finished. He climbed up onto the wagon seat next to Sam who flapped the reins over the backs of the mule team.

"Where to next?" Sam said to Fargo, who scarcely heard him as his thoughts whirled inside his head.

Benny knew everything about their real mission. How could he have found out? Cavendish? Sam? Fargo regarded the man beside him for a moment. Sam was peering down at the mule team before him.

"Should have bought Bessietoo," Sam said as he watched their mule team draw the wagon. "She's a damn good mule. If they had just come down a little on the price. Soon as we finish this trip, I'm going to hightail it back here and rescue her, take her up the trail to El Dorado."

"Sam, you didn't say anything to Benny about our plans, did you?" Fargo asked.

Sam turned pained eyes toward him. Fargo instantly regretted the question.

"You take me for a fool? Why do you ask?"

"Benny knows everything," Skye said. "He hinted as much as I was paying the bill. Cavendish was right. There are no secrets in this town."

Fargo sat in silence and watched the crowded streets. The heat rose in waves. He loosened the bandana around his neck and lowered his hat brim. It sure was hot, more like summer than spring.

As they rounded a corner, he caught sight of the Sweedlers with their painted cart. A crowd had gathered in front.

"These precious sea salts," Maximus Sweedler was saying, "will protect the system from a multitude of infectious diseases . . ."

"Salt!" Sam said sitting bolt upright. "Shoot me if I didn't forget to buy a bag of salt!"

" . . . As well as weakness of the blood, liver, and kidneys. Its speckled gray color is a function of these rare mineral deposits which make it so tasty and so health invoking," Maximus continued.

"How about a bag of Sweedler salts?" Fargo suggested.

Sam reined in the wagon and Fargo hopped down, advancing through the crowd toward the green-suited and fast-talking salesman.

"A five-pound bag of your sea salts," Fargo called out.

"Excellent choice, Mr. Fargo," Sweedler responded. He lowered the back of the trail wagon and leaned inside. Fargo saw dozens of the heavy burlap bags of salt. Sweedler selected one, slit it open at one end and scooped several handfuls into a smaller canvas bag. The mottled gray salts glistened in the sunlight. Sweedler weighed the bag and handed it to Fargo.

"Three dollars," he said. "Expensive, but a pound of prevention is . . ."

"I know, I know," Fargo cut in.

"Good luck on your trail to the fair city of Brotherly Love," Sweedler said in a quiet voice as he pocketed the change.

Fargo felt a wave of shock course through him. Even Maximus Sweedler knew of their mission to Philadelphia? The whole idea of secrecy was a farce!

"Thanks for the salt," Fargo said, moving toward the wagon. He would go to the mint immediately and tell Cavendish the deal was off. Without secrecy, he and Sam would be sitting ducks for the bandits.

Cavendish didn't see it that way.

"Rumors run rampant in this town," Cavendish said. "People are always speculating. Benny and Sweedler were just trying out their own theories to test your reactions. You didn't react, so they will figure they were wrong. Then they will guess that the decoy team is running the gold to Philadelphia."

"I don't like it one bit," Fargo said. "Are you sure you told no one? You sure there hasn't been a leak?"

"Not a chance," Cavendish said.

"Nor with me," Sam said. "Unless I'm talking in my sleep."

"It will blow over," Cavendish said soothingly. "Don't worry about it."

"I still don't like it," Fargo said, unpersuaded.

"Look, Fargo," Cavendish said, his heavy brows coming down over his eyes like a sudden storm. "I'm a careful man. I don't take unnecessary risks. Let me give you an example. A half hour ago, that young woman, Prudence, was in here looking for a job. Now, I'm shorthanded with clerks right now. I know she's a natural with figures. I talked to her in the stagecoach long enough so I have the impression she's a trustworthy young lady. Naturally, I asked her for letters of reference. She said she would have to write back east for them. But, there are three problems. One is she says she needs a job now. She's eager to begin work. Too eager. I don't trust too much eagerness. Second problem is that she gave me the name Smith, Prudence Smith. I don't believe that is her name. Third problem is the company she's keeping."

The picture of Pru and Booth together flashed before Fargo and he nodded slowly. Cavendish had a point about Pru. But he still didn't like the rumors running around Denver City. It would make his job harder. Much harder.

"Okay, Paul. I agree you're a careful man. But your neck's not on the line," Fargo said. "It's Sam and I who will be dodging bullets out on the trail if our real mission is known."

"There's where you're wrong, my friend," Cavendish said. "My neck is right on the line with yours and Sam's. Denver City depends on this mint to attract the gold. We need that new coin press from Philadelphia. This gold shipment has got to get through safely, all thirty thousand dollars of it. The future of the mint depends on that. And, just maybe, the future of Denver City."

In the thoughtful silence that followed Cavendish's speech, Fargo suddenly became aware of someone standing on the other side of the large door of Paul's office. Fargo waited a moment, but there was no knock. Whoever it was, was listening on purpose. He put a finger to his lips and pointed at the door. Then he gestured Cavendish and Sam to talk and prompted them with a question. "So, how do these coins get minted anyway?" he asked.

Cavendish began an explanation of the coin press as Fargo crept toward the door and opened it suddenly.

Laurel stood with her hand poised to knock on the door.

She cried out and tumbled inside. She regained her balance and blushed, twisting her hands nervously on the handle on the basket she carried.

"Laurel!" Cavendish sputtered. "What are you doing here? And why were you listening at the door?"

"I didn't want to interrupt," she said, flustered. "I thought it would be nice if you had a homemade lunch. I packed one and brought it over. I was trying to hear if you were busy and then when I heard Skye's voice, I . . . "

Her face turned beet red and she avoided Fargo's eyes. She was certainly pretty in a delicate kind of way, Fargo thought as he watched her place the basket on Cavendish's desk.

Cavendish rose and put an arm around her.

"How much did you overhear?" he asked gently.

"Enough to know what's going on," she said evenly. Cavendish nodded.

"What do you think of the plan?" he asked her.

"I think it's a risk, but from everything I've heard, Skye could get the gold through if anyone can. And, as for the rumors, you can't stop people from speculating."

"My sentiments exactly," said her father, hugging her close. "Now, what's this talk about a homemade lunch? I knew there was a reason I brought you out west!"

He lifted the cover of the basket. Fargo and Sam rose to leave.

"By the way, Fargo," Paul said, pausing a moment. "The big shindig to send off the decoy—er, gold shipment—team is taking place tonight at Fanny's. I hope you and Sam plan to be there."

Fargo saw Laurel blush again.

"Wouldn't miss it for the world," Fargo said. He and Sam headed back to Fanny's.

Fargo and Sam had just tucked into another full Fanny's special when Matthew Booth walked through the swinging doors and looked slowly around the room. He spotted them and headed toward their table.

Fargo dropped one hand over his Colt and kept himself

relaxed, remembering how tightly wound Booth had been at the stables.

"Mr. Fargo, I presume?" Booth said, halting in front of their table.

"You presume," Fargo said.

He saw Booth's mouth tighten and then force itself into a compressed smile.

"Mind if I join you?" Booth said. "I was in a hurry yesterday when we met. I was less than gracious."

"Somewhat," Fargo said, his voice cool. "Suit yourself." He motioned to an empty chair at the table and Booth sat, calling out for whisky.

Fargo looked carefully at the man before him. Once again, he was struck by the sunken cheeks and eyes, eyes that were brown and would have been handsome if they had not had a hunted, savage look. Booth wasted no time with pleasantries.

"I heard you're planning a prospecting venture," Booth said.

Sam looked up from his drink and shifted uncomfortably. Fargo sighed inwardly. Was this going to be another man telling him that they were really going to Philadephia with the gold but that he wouldn't tell a soul? Did all of Denver City know their plans?

"Word gets around," Fargo said.

"Where do you plan to prospect?" Booth asked as if choosing his words carefully.

Fargo nodded toward Sam.

"I know a hidden place up near Pike's Peak," Sam said. "Virgin stream running through great quartz country. Real promising." Fargo heard the unaffected enthusiasm in Sam's voice.

"Both of you going?" Booth asked.

"What's it to you?" said Fargo.

"Just a friendly question. What's all the secrecy?" Booth asked.

"I just don't like people nosing into my business," Fargo said.

"It's a partnership, to answer your question," Sam said. "We're going together to Pike's Peak."

"Hm," Booth said. "It sounds like a real lucrative venture. I'd like a piece of the action. I'd like to back you."

"We're not looking for backers," Fargo said. "We've already bought our gear and we don't need anything more."

"Never heard of a prospector not interested in a backer," Booth said and Fargo saw a small satisfied smile cross his tight mouth as if he had won something. Booth rose quickly and moved away without another word, taking his seat near the front of the bar, his back to Sam and Fargo as if they had never spoken.

"What was that about?" Sam said.

"Whatever it was, I don't like it," Fargo said, rerunning their conversation in his mind. Booth had found out what he wanted to know. But what had it been?

"He may be the only person in Denver City who doesn't know we're not prospecting," Sam said in a very quiet voice.

"Or is pretending not to know," Fargo said. "The question is, why?"

4

"Drinks are on the house," the black-vested bartender said, pushing the Taos Lightning across the mahogany bar toward Skye.

Skye took it and downed it, felt the jagged edge cut through his innards. It wasn't the kind of drink you could sip.

The bartenders were hopping back and forth like nervous chickens, refilling drinks, while Fanny and her girls hefted huge platters of grub from the kitchen to the tables at one end of the wide room. From the look of things, just about everybody in Denver City was jammed into the room. People could hardly move, much less dance. Fargo stood at one end of the bar watching the party, and nursing his doubts about Paul Cavendish.

Cavendish had delivered what he promised—it was one helluva shindig in honor of Wyatt Roundtree and the team of men departing the next day with what everybody was supposed to think was the gold shipment. Even Roundtree didn't know that he was a decoy. That's the way Cavendish wanted it.

Fargo glanced around the packed room wondering which young man was Wyatt Roundtree. He had a reputation as an ambitious upstart, cocksure and full of himself. Fargo was certain he'd run into him. He sounded like the kind you always ran into.

Fargo watched Cavendish cross the room to welcome more guests. He was beginning to suspect that Cavendish was not as savvy as he had first thought. For one thing, the big party for Roundtree was supposed to draw the attention of any conspirators. But it would look suspicious to somebody really smart and bent on stealing the gold. A conspirator would figure that Cavendish would send a gold shipment off quietly.

And Cavendish wasn't even worried that Benny and Sweedler knew that Fargo and Sam would carry the gold. Hell, if a shopkeeper and a snake-oil salesman knew their secret, then the rest of the town knew as well.

He'd been hired to move the gold out of Denver City as instructed, Fargo told himself. If Cavendish couldn't see the warning signs, then Fargo couldn't answer for the consequences. He'd do his best on the trail.

A crowd of prospectors, with their wide hats and sunbleached beards hung over the bar opening their buckskin pokes to pay for drinks. Sweeteye Sam had joined a noisy card game with Benny and two cowpokes. Booth had joined another card game with a slick looking gambling man and two soldiers from nearby Camp Weld. Pru stood behind him watching over his shoulder.

"Wyatt!" Fargo heard a female voice say and he turned to see who was being called.

A young man with clean straight features and an intense gaze tipped his hat toward the woman. He was swaggering as he made his way through the crowd toward the bar, Fargo noted. This was Wyatt Roundtree's big night. Roundtree ordered a drink with an oversized gesture and when the bartender handed him a beer, he turned and caught sight of Fargo watching. Wyatt made his way over.

"Name's Roundtree," he said, extending his hand grandly. "Course, you probably know that already." All the attention was going to his head.

"Skye Fargo."

Roundtree's eyebrows shot up and suspicion filled his eyes.

"I've heard your name before," he said, rubbing his smooth chin. "But I can't remember where."

Fargo looked at him. The kid wasn't yet twenty.

"Real important job you got here," Fargo said. He tried to suppress a smile as he thought of what Wyatt Roundtree would say when he got to Philadelphia and found out he wasn't carrying gold ingots, but lead bars instead. Wouldn't that take Wyatt Roundtree down a peg?

"Very important job," Roundtree agreed, keeping his face

long. "I told Mr. Cavendish I'd get the gold safely to Philadelphia or die trying!"

"Then you're the right man for the job," Fargo said, with an inward chuckle. Roundtree nodded, pleased by the compliment, and moved off.

Fargo felt a soft hand on his arm and turned to see Prudence standing beside him. Her glossy brown hair cascaded over her shoulders, one curl escaping to rest in the deep cleavage between her round breasts which pushed up above the low neck of her dress.

"Jumpin' jubilee!" she said. "Some party, isn't it?"

Fargo looked at her and didn't answer. She squirmed slightly under his silent gaze.

"Look, I'm sorry I was so testy the other day," she said after a moment's awkward pause.

Fargo remained silent, waiting to hear what else she would say.

"This deal with Cavendish you're cooking up . . ."

"What's that supposed to mean?" he cut in. Who *didn't* know their secret?

"Oh, I just heard some rumors," she answered. "But Skye, there's something I have to tell you. Cavendish is not to be trusted."

"And where did you hear that rumor?" Fargo asked her. "From Matthew Booth?"

"Yes, as a matter of fact," Pru said.

"I've heard Matthew Booth is a crook. He was fired from the mint for having his hand in the till."

"He was innocent!" Pru exclaimed and Fargo saw tears suddenly well up in her eyes.

"How do you know that?" Fargo asked.

"I just know," Pru said.

"Because Booth told you?" Fargo pressed.

"Not just that. You see, Matthew Booth is . . ."

Just then three shots rang out in close succession. Fargo wheeled and drew his Colt in one fluid motion. Booth was standing at the card table, his carved silver revolver smoking in one hand. The gambling man lay on the floor groaning, holding his leg which sprouted blood onto the floor.

"Take the ace out of your sleeve, Kincaid," Booth hissed

to the man, "or you'll get some lead in your other leg too."

As he advanced toward the table, Fargo heard Fanny's voice.

"Go fetch Doc Fletcher," she said to one of her girls as she bustled toward the man writhing on the floor. "And the sheriff."

"Holster it, Booth," Fargo said, covering him with his Colt.

"This man was cheating," Booth said. "And he's getting a double helping of lead unless I see that ace up his sleeve right now." Booth cocked his pistol.

There was no one standing behind Booth. Fargo pulled the trigger and Booth's pistol flew from his hand.

"Son of a bitch!" he screamed, holding his stung hand under his arm.

Fargo kept his Colt trained on Booth and glanced at the table. He saw large piles of chips, gold coins and buckskin pokes in front of three places and very few in front of Booth's chair. Clearly, Booth had been losing all evening.

"How do you know Kincaid was cheating?" Fargo asked.

"There was an ace missing from the deck," Booth answered. "I was counting. There are three cards remaining in the draw. None of them is an ace. So, he's got it up his sleeve."

"That's ridiculous," Kincaid groaned. "I play fair and square. Ask anybody." Fanny knelt beside Kincaid, removed the silk handkerchief from his pocket and hastily applied a tourniquet to his leg, using a fork to turn it to stop the flow of blood.

"That's right," said one of the prospectors, nodding vigorously. "I've played Kincaid lots of times. He's a sharp card player but he's not a cheat."

Fargo leaned over and unbuttoned Kincaid's vest. Inside were two pockets and he slid his fingers into each of them. No cards.

"Unbutton your sleeves," he said to Kincaid. Fanny helped him, rolling back the cuffs, but there were no cards there either.

"Any other ideas?" Fargo said to Booth.

"He was cheating!" Booth insisted petulantly.

Fargo reached over and picked up the three cards lying in a pile face down in the center of the table. He turned them over and spread them out face up. A queen, a three and the ace of diamonds.

"That the ace?" Fargo asked Booth.

Booth's mouth dropped open for a moment.

"He must have inserted it back into the deck!" Booth sputtered in a rage. "These gambling cheats can do that, you know."

"You miscounted the cards!" yelled Kincaid. "The goddamn diamond ace was never played. It was in the deck the whole time!"

"I never saw the fourth ace come up," one of the prospectors mumbled under his breath, agreeing with Kincaid.

Fargo heard a rustle in the room as Doc Fletcher pushed through the crowd. Fanny moved aside as Doc knelt over Kincaid.

"Good tourniquet," he muttered as he carefully pulled back the torn fabric from around the bullet wound. He stood up quickly.

"You two men help me carry him across the street," Doc said. "Give us a couple of bottles of whisky, Fanny. Kincaid will need some help when I start fishing those bullets out of his leg."

The crowd parted as they moved Kincaid out of the room. They passed the sheriff who was coming in the door.

"Bad card game, Fanny?" the sheriff asked her as he approached. He eyed Fargo suspiciously, lowering his bushy black eyebrows.

"It's this one, Sheriff," Fanny said, nodding toward Booth. Fargo saw Pru sidle up to stand next to the tall angry man.

"Oh, Mr. Booth," the sheriff said familiarly. "This is the fourth complaint I've had about you in as many days. You'll have to spend the night in jail."

"But this isn't fair!" Prudence said suddenly. "That man Kincaid was cheating!"

"Somebody want to tell me what's going on?" the sheriff asked.

"According to Booth, Kincaid had an ace up his sleeve. But, he didn't have any cards hidden on him and the ace was still on the table," Fargo explained.

"You fellas agree with that?" the sheriff asked the prospectors.

They nodded and one of them said, "Booth was just sore because he's been losing all night."

"That's not fair!" Pru said.

"Let's go, Booth," the sheriff said. He took Booth by the arm and escorted him from the room. Fanny called for one of the bartenders to clean up the mess and within a few moments, the party resumed as if nothing had happened.

Fargo saw Pru standing in the same place looking in the direction of the door.

"I'd watch out for that Booth character," he said to her.

"Don't you say one word against him!" she said, fury blazing in her brown eyes. She turned on her heel and made her way toward the doors.

There was just no figuring out women, Fargo thought. Prudence had seemed a reasonable sort. But her defense of Matthew Booth was downright crazy. Fargo walked over toward the table where Sam was playing poker. And winning, Fargo noted.

In between hands, Fargo leaned over and said in a low voice to Sam, "What's the odds that Booth was being cheated?"

"One in a million," Sam said. "If that."

Fargo nodded. "That's about what I figured," he said.

It was like the story of the mint, he thought. Matthew Booth denied he had skimmed gold from the mint, despite all evidence to the contrary. And a lot of people believed him. And tonight, there still remained the possibility, however remote, that Kincaid had managed to slip an ace back into the deck—or that Kincaid had a deck with two diamond aces. Well, if Booth was honest, he was the unluckiest honest man Fargo had ever encountered. And the nastiest.

"Attention ladies and gentlemen!" Paul Cavendish said above the noise, climbing onto a chair as the room quieted. "Attention!"

For the second time that evening, Fargo felt a woman's

hand on his arm. Laurel smiled up at him, the light of the chandelier making a pale gold halo of her sleek blond hair. Fargo smiled back.

" . . . to propose a toast to Wyatt Roundtree and these fine fellows," Cavendish was saying, "who will be responsible for the safety of the new coin press. These men will make it possible for Denver City—and the mint—to become the Queen of the West!"

Cavendish raised his glass, as did everyone in the room. Whoops and cheers followed. Somebody fired a pistol in all the excitement and the chandelier suddenly crashed onto a table, scattering the card game in progress. Chaos ensued.

"Let's get out of here," Fargo said, taking Laurel's elbow and guiding her the short distance through the batwing doors and out into the cool night air. They walked along the deserted boardwalk, their heels making a hollow sound. She shivered and drew her shawl around her.

"It was such a hot day for spring, and now the night is so cold."

"It's the thin air," Fargo said, suppressing the desire to put his arm around her. "Don't forget that Denver City is a mile high. The air just doesn't hold the heat of the day very long. This too cold for you?"

"It's bracing," she said. "Let's walk down to the Larimer Street bridge."

They reached Cherry Creek, and walked halfway across the wooden bridge that had just been completed a few months before, the lumber still raw and yellow. There was no moon. By the pale starlight he could see the creek bed. Cherry Creek was usually a trickle of water winding across a flat plain of sand between steep banks. Tonight there was a heavy current. Fargo leaned over the railing to gauge the depth.

"Never seen that much water in Cherry Creek," he murmured almost to himself. "Must be the spring runoff."

"When I was in Boston this past winter, father's letters were full of news about how much snow there was. A very heavy winter," Laurel said.

Fargo looked down at the dark waters swirling beneath the bridge.

"Somebody'd better keep an eye on Cherry Creek for the next few days."

"Surely the water couldn't get as high as the banks," Laurel said, eyeing the low cliffs on either side. She shivered again. Again, Fargo was tempted to put his arm around her, but hesitated, considering her age.

"If the snowmelt's heavy enough, it could."

Laurel tossed her long blond hair back over one shoulder, smiled at Fargo and then looked out at the water. She seemed to be waiting for him to make a move. She was beautiful, he thought. Beautiful in the way starlight was, fragile and pure, but strangely powerful. The night breeze lifted her hair about her face and made the fringe on her shawl dance. Again he admired her slender waist. He remembered how light she had been when he had lifted her down from the stagecoach.

"You . . ."

"I . . ."

They both spoke at the same moment, and then hesitated and laughed.

"You first," Fargo said.

"I was just going to say I've never met anyone like you. You are an unusual man," Laurel said, smiling up at him, her gray eyes steady in the starlight, her lips soft and full.

"How so?" God, she was lovely. He could feel a pleasurable ache beginning in him and he longed to take her in his arms.

"You step in when people are in trouble. Like that gambler who was shot by Booth. You take control and clear things up. I like that in a person."

Fargo thought she was giving him the benefit of the doubt. There were a lot of questions in his mind about this job, about Booth and about Cavendish. He wished he could just step right in, clear things up. He wished things were as simple as that this time. But, he was glad she had confidence in him.

"Comes from a life on the trail. You watch everything. Question everything. Trust nothing. Then when the moment comes, you act. There's no second chance," he said, thinking of the moment when he might seize her in his arms, cradle her head in his hands, bend her backward and kiss her, kiss her neck, kiss her . . .

"And what were you going to say?" she asked. He saw her breasts rise and fall. She was breathing quickly. Her wide eyes stayed on his as if drinking him in.

"I was about to say the same thing about you," he said. "You are an unusual woman. Intelligent. Independent. Beautiful." He could feel himself drawn to her and he stepped forward, folding her into his arms.

She raised her face to his and her soft lips parted even before he kissed her. He felt the caged desire for her exploding inside him and felt her tremble as he gently inserted his tongue between her lips, probing and teasing. Her hands were around his neck, removing his hat and dropping it on the bridge, entwining her fingers in his hair, tickling his ears and neck, and she was breathing hard as they kissed more passionately, with greater urgency. He backed her up against the railing and felt her press her firm breasts against him. He was hard and swollen and she felt that too, shifting her hips to let him know that it was welcome. Through his Levi's and beneath the folds of her dress he felt her soft mound of pleasure.

"Oh, Skye," she gasped, breathless, as the long kiss broke. "I've wanted you since the moment you lifted me down from the coach."

"I wasn't sure I should make a move," he said. "I didn't want to scare you off."

"Did I act scared?"

"Well, you blushed a lot."

"I thought you could see how I felt. I wasn't sure you felt the same way."

"Glad that's cleared up," he said and kissed her again and again, tenderly, in a long trail down her pale neck, inhaling the clean lemony smell of her, and nuzzling down her chest until he reached the soft swells of her breasts. Her chest rose and fell as she panted. He could feel her trying to hold herself back.

"Laurel! Laurel!"

She started and pulled away as she heard her father call. "Shit!" she said.

Fargo laughed in surprise as he heard her swear and leaned down to pick up his hat.

"Excuse my language," she said in a quiet voice to Fargo. "I'm here, Father!" she called out.

"What are you doing out on the bridge?" Cavendish

called. Fargo heard the anger and fear in his voice as his footsteps approached on the wooden span.

"I'm with Fargo," she said.

"Oh," he said, as he drew near. "That's a relief. I started worrying when I couldn't find you at the party. Nobody had seen you leave, so I thought I'd better look around."

"I'm sorry," Laurel said. "I should have told you we were taking a walk."

Cavendish nodded and pulled a cigar from his vest pocket, snipped one end and lit it, puffed for a moment and looked out over Cherry Creek.

"Hmm. Water's awfully high tonight," he observed. "It could flood if it gets higher. I'll tell some of the men tomorrow morning."

"I had the same thought," Fargo said. There was an awkward pause. Fargo wondered if Cavendish had guessed that something was going on between Laurel and him. Fargo could almost hear Laurel thinking of a way to ask her father to go back to the party alone, but after a moment, it was clear she couldn't find one.

"We'd best be getting back to Fanny's," she said. Fargo heard the slight reluctance in her voice, put there so that he would hear it and know that they would find another opportunity soon, know that she was willing and wanting.

"Actually, the party's just breaking up. Shall we turn in?" Cavendish said, offering his arm to his daughter. He had a second thought. "Or perhaps Fargo could bring you home later?" he asked delicately.

To Fargo's surprise, Laurel accepted her father's arm and said, "It is getting late."

Fargo walked them to their home on Curtis Street, a large white house with a columned portico. As Fargo said goodnight, Laurel gave him her hand and squeezed his. She was obviously unsure of herself as a woman in front of her father. Well, she was still very young.

Fargo walked back to Fanny's where the girls and the bartender were mopping up. Fanny emerged from the kitchen, untying her apron.

"Great party, Fanny," Fargo said.

"Sure made one helluva mess, but I'd do it again for

Paul Cavendish," she said. "Where'd you run off to?"

"I took a turn around town with Laurel," Fargo said nonchalantly.

Fanny's eyebrows shot up.

"Girls grow up fast in these parts," she said. "But you'd be good for Laurel." She nodded and looked Fargo over from hat to boots. "Yes, you'll do just fine," she said.

Fargo grinned. He had a feeling Fanny had some sway over Cavendish. That might be useful in the next couple of days, he thought as he climbed the stairs.

Booth's eyes narrowed and flashed an angry red.

"You can't fool me," he said. "I know all about the gold."

He was shuffling a deck of cards and, as he moved his hand, Fargo saw that one of his wrists was in shackles. A chain led downward. On the floor, chained to the other end was Pru, blindfolded. Tears seeped out from underneath the black cloth binding her eyes. Each tear, as it rolled down her cheek splashed on the floor. Fargo was ankle deep in water. He looked again at the deck of cards and watched Booth's hands turn up the ace of diamonds.

"It's important that you trust me," the man said, and Fargo saw that Booth had turned into Cavendish.

"I trust you," Fargo heard himself say, and he saw Laurel standing behind her father looking over his shoulder. She looked up at Fargo, smiled and then her eye fixed on something just behind him and she screamed. Fargo wheeled and tried to draw, but there was no Colt in his holster. His hand grasped nothing.

The bronzed Arapaho warrior with the iridescent feather stood behind him, tomahawk raised toward the sky. Fargo realized the Indian was not threatening him, merely lifting his weapon up in some kind of prayer.

Pru's tears were flooding the room. Fargo's knees were wet and he could hear the running water.

The warrior looked down at him and said, "When the mountains are green, we will come again."

Fargo awoke with his heart racing, the Indian's words echoing in his ears. He rubbed his face to dispell the dream, remembering the Arapaho tribe moving their camp. The

74

words the warrior had spoken on the trail came back to him now.

"When the mountains are green . . ."

The mountains were white. It was late spring and the high country still slept under a blanket of snow from the winter, Fargo thought.

Suddenly he heard a noise like an explosion, the sound of running water and wood splintering, a woman's scream and men shouting. No dream. These sounds were real.

He sprang up immediately from the bed, pulling on his clothes and buttoning his shirt as he ran down the stairs, cursing himself.

Of course! The Arapaho could read the signs better than anyone. On the front range of the Rocky Mountains was a heavy layer of snow which the hot spring days were melting, making the perfect condition for a flash flood. The Arapaho had moved their camp away from the banks of Cherry Creek until the mountains were green—that is until the snow had melted away.

Fargo cursed himself again for not figuring out what the warrior had been trying to tell him. He pushed through the doors out onto the street and ran toward the bridge.

As he passed the stable, he realized he would need rope. Fargo ducked into the dark stable and took the lariat from his saddle. His pinto smelled him and nickered, then stamped his feet nervously. The horse heard and smelled the flood and didn't want to be trapped. Fargo saddled the Ovaro, mounted, and galloped down to the creek.

Cherry Creek was a wild torrent of black water. The Larimer Street Bridge listed to one side, about to topple into the swirling waters. Three paralyzed figures clung to the railings. The woman was screaming with fear and the two men shouted for help.

Near the three was an upright piling which supported the bridge. Fargo quickly tied a lasso and swung it over his head, releasing it so that the wavering loop arced out over the dark waters and fell around the piling, catching one of the men too. Fargo pulled the lariat tight as the man adjusted it to the piling. He pulled the rope at an angle so that it served as a railing over the teetering bridge. Fargo tied the other end of the rope around his saddle pommel.

"Hold on to the rope and don't look down," Fargo shouted to the woman. She was bulky and unsure of herself. She would not be able to negotiate the bridge easily.

"I can't!" he heard her scream, but one of the men took her hands from around the railing, locked them onto the rope and gave her a push.

Fargo dismounted and approached the end of the half-fallen bridge. He walked out a few steps, holding on to the rope. The woman had not moved more than a step. She was petrified. Her checkered dress was soaked and clung to her ample frame. Even in the dim starlight, he could see that her teeth were chattering.

"Hold on to the rope. You won't fall," Fargo yelled above the roaring water.

His voice caught her attention and she looked up at him, sudden hope on her face.

"That's it!" he encouraged. "One step at a time."

She made a few tentative steps. He eased himself carefully out onto the bridge toward her.

"Get one foot planted. Then move the other one," he shouted. She looked up at him for an instant and smiled like a small girl.

Just then a swell of water hit the bridge and it swayed dangerously. Fargo caught himself against the railing and watched in horror as the woman lost her footing on the wet wooden bridge and swung out over the swirling stream, holding on to the rope. The Ovaro took a step forward and then adjusted his stance to hold the rope taut. The woman held on and screamed in terror.

Fargo cursed and moved toward her, the bridge threatening to topple under his weight. Just as he reached her, her strength gave out and she lost her grip on the rope. Fargo reached for her at the same instant and closed his hand around one of her wrists, digging his fingers into her cold flesh. She hung down, her body dangling above the flood.

Fargo summoned up black anger—anger at this flood, anger at innocent people in needless anger, anger at himself for not reading the signs of the flash flood—and the anger coalesced into a wave of energy as he lifted her upward onto the bridge. She gasped hysterically and he lifted her again, throwing her over one shoulder so that he could carry her ashore.

He held the rope with one hand, moving slowly across the groaning timbers and placed her unceremoniously on the ground beside the Ovaro and she began sobbing. He turned his attention back to the two men on the bridge. In a few moments the first man moved across the creaking bridge to shore. The second one began to cross, holding on to the rope.

"Tie the rope around your waist!" Fargo instructed him. The heavy-set man did so. Then he began to make his way to the shore holding on to the railing, while the Ovaro backed up the slope to keep the rope taut.

Upstream, Fargo heard the roar of an approaching wall of water. He saw a dark mass moving toward the bridge. The man heard it too and hurried. The roaring wave hit the pilings of the bridge. The lumber gave way in a deafening explosion of groaning timbers and splintering wood as the bridge tilted and then toppled into the dark chaos of the flood. Fargo saw the man grasp the railing and then plummet into the water as the bridge broke up.

Fargo seized the rope and pulled, feeling the weight of the man jerking on the other end. He was probably caught under something, perhaps broken sections of the span. Fargo pulled on the rope but could not get it to budge. He searched among the floating debris for any sign of the man, but saw nothing.

Holding the rope in his left hand, Fargo plunged into the raging current. His body contracted in the icy grip of the water which had been snow only hours before. He took a deep breath and dove beneath the surface, following the rope downward hand over hand.

An eddy caught him. He felt a sharp blow to the side of his head. A log or piece of lumber had careened into him. His eyes were closed, but he saw points of dancing lights like stars burning behind his eyelids, and he almost lost his grip. Again the black rage came. His hand tightened on the rope. Anger radiated from the iron grip, warming him, energizing his arms, clearing his head, and giving him renewed strength. He continued downward, pushing away branches entangled in the rope, ignoring the burning of his lungs.

A moment later, he felt the knot tied around a soft belly. He felt about and found a heavy beam lying across the man's legs. The man didn't move, but he hadn't been under the water long enough to drown.

Fargo clamped down his jaw and knelt on the rocky bottom of the stream, wrapping one of his knees through the rope. He braced one shoulder beneath the beam and pushed, feeling his muscles, contracted from the cold, strain against the weight. The beam shifted, then moved enough for Fargo to ease the man out.

Skye's head was beginning to whirl and he fought the desire to inhale the water. His lungs ached, desperate for air. He jerked on the rope three times and felt the pony start forward, felt himself and the man being pulled through the tangled branches and cold swirling waters toward the air—air.

Fargo gasped as his head broke the surface. Then he coughed, drinking in burning draughts of the cold night air. He felt weary, desperate for rest. He shook the feeling away and, hooking his arm around the man, dragged him up the bank.

The man was cold and silent. Fargo shook him hard, then turned him over, opened his mouth and beat him on the back to expel the water. He shook him again and then laid him out, pushing up and down on his chest, hearing the cold air pump in and out of the man's still form. Fargo cursed, pushed on his chest again and again until he heard a rib crack. He shifted the position of his hands. The man finally sputtered and coughed. Fargo sat him up and grasped him from behind, continuing to pump the air into his lungs, until he felt the man's breathing begin. It was erratic, but he would live. The other man and the woman climbed down the bank to join Fargo.

"How can we thank you?" the man asked.

"Drag him farther up the bank in case there's another surge," Fargo said.

Fargo stood and looked about. The wall of water which had washed out the bridge had destroyed dozens of the buildings closest to the creek. He could see the foundations where some of them had been swept away and others hung precariously over the eroded banks.

The water was full of swirling debris. He saw the occasional body of a drowned sheep. The flood had brought

78

out the Denver City citizens. They lined the banks, milling in confusion.

Fargo tried to think of how to organize a rescue effort. People were undoubtedly being swept by even as he stood there, he told himself. He couldn't swim after them all. It was hopeless. He could only save a few.

He took a step forward and stumbled. His toe was caught in a cable from the fallen bridge. Fargo bent down to untangle his leg and saw that the wire plunged into the stream. He tugged on it, but it was fastened securely, running into the water and across the torrent. He had an idea.

He raced up the bank and saw Cavendish pacing up and down.

"Paul, we have a chance to save some people," Fargo said. "I need twenty men fast." In an instant, several dozen men followed Fargo down to the edge of the water.

"Hook the cable through your belts," he instructed them. "Fan out in a long line across the stream. The wire is loose, so you'll float down and form a wide V. Keep the wire clear. Don't let anything get trapped. Keep your eyes open for anybody who's fallen in. Pass them man to man toward shore. The ones in the middle will have the hardest job, so you'll have to rotate."

The men grasped the plan instantly and immediately lined up, unbuckling their belts and rebuckling them around the cable. The wire was tangled with debris and it took some time to clear it. But halfway across, they found a young boy clinging to a portion of a roof trapped in an island of flotsam.

At least the people who fell in upstream of the bridge would have a chance to be saved. Fargo turned his thoughts downstream. He left Cavendish in charge of the rescue line, wound up his rope, mounted and climbed up the bank.

There were women and children at the top, looking down at the raging river. A bonfire was burning and more were being started to give light to the rescue operations and to provide warmth for rescued victims. The three people he had saved from the bridge sat beside the fire. Laurel bent over the fat man who had almost drowned, giving him a cup of something hot, and adjusting a blanket around him.

She looked up when she heard the pinto.

"Skye! Where are you going?" she shouted.

"Heading downstream," he said. "A lot of people have already been swept by. I hope to find some."

"I'll come too," Laurel said. "Father," she shouted down to Cavendish. "I'm going with Fargo."

Cavendish turned and waved to let her know he heard, then directed his attention back to the effort to bring in a half-drowned woman, who had been found holding on to a log. Laurel noticed Fargo's wet clothes and she grabbed a blanket from one of the women.

"Use this," she said firmly. Fargo wrapped it around him as he sat on the horse. He removed his foot from the stirrup so that she could use it to mount, and gave her a hand up. She swung up behind him and put her arms around his waist. She was not coy, he noticed.

The surefooted pinto moved swiftly along the creek's edge. By the starlight, Fargo scanned the banks and saw the flood's destruction—collapsed houses, eroded banks, the piles of branches strewn everywhere, bodies of animals on the banks. Here and there were knots of people with ropes, rescuing families clinging to parts of their homes.

A mile downstream, where the buildings were sparse, Fargo heard a baby crying and a child's voice calling for help.

"Do you hear that?" Laurel asked.

Fargo didn't answer but spurred the Ovaro down to the edge of the boiling water. Halfway across the river he saw the edge of a pale sandbar and a dark tangle of branches. Something white fluttered.

"I'm going across," he said as he dismounted.

He tied one end of the rope to the saddle pommel and, wrapping the other end around one hand, he leapt into the water, hoping he would not encounter any submerged logs when he landed. His body adjusted to the icy water quickly this time. He struck out toward the sandbar, using the girl's plaintive voice as a beacon.

His muscular arms fought the current and he swam with long strokes, pushing away floating logs. He felt the sandy bottom rise and he emerged, dripping, and shook the water from his eyes.

The fluttering he had seen from the shore was a tiny hand-kerchief tied to a branch. The girl's voice continued to cry for help, over and over.

"I'm here," he said.

He heard a rustle and he moved forward. Sitting among the branches, like a small bedraggled sparrow, was a girl of about six years old, her wet hair plastered to her head. In her arms was an infant and beside her huddled a small boy, who looked at Fargo with wide, frightened eyes.

"I heard you calling me," he said gently to the little girl.

"I knew you would," she said. "Did my pa send you?"

"Yes," he lied. He looked at the three of them for a moment. He would have to make two trips.

"Are you alright?" he asked her.

"Cold," she said, and he saw that she was trying to keep her teeth from chattering. Plucky kid. Fargo secured one end of the rope onto a heavy log to use for the return trip.

"I'm going to take your brother first," he decided. "Then I'll come right back." She nodded bravely and pushed the small boy in Fargo's direction. The boy hung back, afraid.

"I'm taking you to ride on my horse. He's waiting on the bank," Fargo said, pointing across the water. The boy nodded. "First we have to swim. Get on my shoulders. Keep your eye on my horse."

They made the crossing quickly and when they approached the bank, Fargo handed the boy up to Laurel and swam across again. He made the second trip the same way, but more slowly with the girl atop his shoulders with the infant in her arms.

Just as they neared the bank, he heard Laurel shout a warning and he saw a huge dark log looming, heading toward them. Fargo moved forward, grasping one of the girl's legs with one hand, holding one end of the rope with the other. The log crashed into them, glancing painfully off his shoulder. He kept a hold on the girl.

"Bobby! Bobby!" the little girl screamed.

Fargo saw the bundled baby land in the water and, almost instantaneously, he heard a splash. He knew it was Laurel diving into the water. He pushed his way to the shore and lifted the sobbing girl onto the bank, turning immediately to swim after Laurel. She was nowhere to be seen.

5

Fargo scanned the dark surges of muddy water, swirling and eddying with the power of a cataract. Moments passed and he heard a roaring in his ears as his eyes roved anxiously over the dark waves. There was no use diving in if he didn't know which direction to swim. Still, with each passing second, Laurel and the baby were being swept farther downstream. Or, worse yet, they might be underwater, entangled in submerged branches.

Just as he was about to dive in anyway, Laurel's arms broke the surface of the water, one hand held over the infant's mouth and nose, the other holding up the little body. Good instincts, Fargo thought in the instant it took for him to dive into the raging waters. Not old enough to hold its breath, the baby would have sucked in enough water to drown if Laurel hadn't covered its mouth and nose. Now she could only bob up and down, unable to swim for shore as she held the baby aloft.

His powerful arms, aided by the current, swept him toward Laurel. He reached out and hooked her waist with his arm, pulling her toward shore and dragging them up the bank. Laurel shook her head to clear it. She was disoriented. Then she realized she still held her hand tightly over the baby's face, which was dark colored. She let go instantly and the baby gave a sputter and then a yell. Fargo grinned at her as she looked up.

"Nice dive," he said. "They teach you swimming in Boston too?"

Laurel nodded. Then suddenly her face contorted and she was sobbing, holding the crying child in her arms. Fargo put his arms around her.

"I was . . . so . . . frightened," she said between sobs, burying her head against his chest. The child squalled.

"That makes three of us," he murmured, kissing her wet hair.

After a moment, her crying subsided and she patted the child until he had quieted.

"Let's get back to the other two," Fargo said.

As they walked back upstream, Fargo heard the girl's pitiful voice crying for help over and over again.

"We're coming!" he called.

"With the baby!" Laurel yelled. She was shivering. The infant's cries had subsided to whimpers. He would have to get these kids warm immediately.

"We'll need to light a fire," he said when they came to the pinto.

Fargo hurried to gather dry wood and moss and soon had a roaring fire going on a high knoll. While he gathered an extra supply of wood, Laurel undressed the three children, dried them and wrapped them together in the blanket, where they fell asleep almost instantly. She squeezed out their clothes and hung them to dry beside the flames.

"You ought to get out of your wet things too," Fargo said to her. The soggy dress clinging to her legs was beginning to steam in the heat from the fire.

She unbuttoned her dress and let it slip down around her, leaving her in a lacy petticoat which clung to her curves. She kept her eyes on the ground.

"I've got my bedroll on my saddle if you want to get some sleep," Fargo offered.

"I suddenly don't want to sleep," Laurel said, glancing up at him. "But the bedroll might be useful."

Fargo smiled.

Laurel slipped one strap of her petticoat off her shoulder. The lace slipped downward and in the flickering firelight Fargo saw her firm pale breast, perfectly shaped, the tip a pale pink. Laurel was smiling at his expression.

"How about if I build another campfire, say, within earshot? In case they wake up?" he asked her, nodding toward the sleeping children.

"How about your wet things?" she said.

"Fire first," he said, retrieving the bedroll from his saddle and selecting a protected clearing. He quickly laid a second campfire, spread out the bedroll and returned to where Laurel stood. She was arranging her dress and her bloomers across several branches to dry and still wore the wet slip.

She turned when she heard his steps and he swept her up in his strong arms, carrying her toward the other campfire, while she clung to him.

He put her down to stand beside the crackling fire and kissed her deeply, his tongue filling her mouth, exploring her sweetness. She broke off and stepped back, lowering the other strap of her slip and exposing both her firm small breasts, round and inviting, the pale pink nipples crinkled and erect in the cold night air. She pulled the slip down gently so that it fell around her feet and he saw the firelight glisten in the short fur of the pale gold triangle between her long slender legs.

Fargo unbuttoned his shirt quickly, then lowered his Levi's, tossing them onto rocks near the fire and keeping his eyes on her, drinking in the sight of her fragile pale loveliness.

He picked her up, kissed her again and again deeply as her slender arms clung to him and he turned around under the early morning stars, feeling the world whirl about them while he held her willowy warmth fast against him, safe from the dark waters.

Then he lowered her gently onto the bedroll where she stretched out. He cupped his hand around one breast and kissed the other, burying his face against its softness. Then he kissed her belly, downward as she panted, until he came to the golden tangle. He gently nuzzled the mound and slowly, very slowly, placed the tip of his tongue lightly at the top of the lips. He could taste her delicate musky sweetness, like spring wine, and he heard her moan.

He held her hips in both hands and gently opened her thighs, taking her wetness into his mouth, rolling the tender flesh between his own lips and stroking her with his tongue.

"Please, please," she moaned. "Yes."

He flicked his tongue across her slipperiness and then,

pointed it and gently inserted it, moving his head from side to side as she writhed with pleasure. He felt her shifting her body across the bedroll. He paused for a moment, then felt her cup her hand under him, stroking his hardness with her soft hand. Then she shifted and he felt her wet on him, taking him into her mouth, her tongue stroking the shaft again and again, wet and tight on him. And he plunged his tongue into her again, opening his mouth wide to take all of her inside at once, feeling himself inside her at the same moment, wetness and an infinite number of pleasurable sensations, as if a rainbow exploded.

He sucked on her swollen lips and felt the small hard button of her suddenly contract as she shuddered, her thighs coming together and she moaned, her mouth full of him, pulling on him, her tongue darting across the delicate head.

"Stop, stop," he said, but she moaned and continued until he could not hold back any longer and the night exploded, colors rising before his eyes and falling down over them in a showering spectrum of pleasure and forgetfulness.

After a moment, he sat up and kissed her breasts again, and her mouth, gently. She lay with her gray eyes half closed, watching him and smiling.

"Don't tell me you learned that in a Boston girls' school," he said.

"Let's just say I had a liberal education," she answered and she pulled him down toward her, taking him again in her hand, surprised to find him ready for her so soon, and guiding him inside her. He pushed inside her warm tightness, slowly, slowly, kissing her forehead and her face gently, until she could bear it no longer and began moving her hips faster, rhythmically against his and they came again together, as if falling in slow motion, and relaxed into dark sleep.

Fargo awoke and saw the first streaks of light on the eastern horizon. He gently removed his arm from under Laurel's head and rose quietly, throwing another log on the coals of the campfire and blowing on it to make it flare. He dressed in his clothes which the fire-warm rocks had dried during the night. Laurel's slip lay in a heap on the ground, still damp, and he hung it over a branch by the quickening flames, then crept toward the other campfire which had burned down to embers. The three children were still sleeping and Fargo put a few thick branches on the fire which was soon crackling.

From his saddlebags, he fished out a thin coffee pot, coffee and some hardtack. At least it would be something, he thought.

The coffee was ready and the pieces of hardtack lay on a rock, when he heard Laurel's footsteps.

"Good morning, sleepy head," he greeted her, as she stole forward in her slip.

She kissed him, slid into her dress and leaned over the children. The baby stirred. Laurel took him up and the little girl awoke. Fargo left her alone to dress them and went to put out the other campfire.

When he returned, Laurel and the two children were dressed and dipping the hardtack into the coffee. The baby was crying. They would have to get back quickly to find it some milk.

By the time the sun was over the horizon, they had broken camp, loaded the children onto the horse and were making their way back to Denver City, striking out across the buffalo grass.

"Isn't it easier to go along the creek?" Laurel asked.

"It is," Fargo answered. "But I'm afraid we might see a lot of dead animals and who knows what else on that route. The less these kids see right now, the better."

"Right," Laurel agreed. "I asked the children their names and they said Morton. I remember Father talking about Wayne and Emily Morton. I hope they're still alive. I wouldn't want to see these three orphaned."

"I'm afraid we're going to see a lot of things we don't want to see when we get back to Denver City," Fargo said.

By the time they entered town, it was crackling with energy, with people running to and fro. The streets were crowded with wagons going down to the river to haul away the debris. Fargo saw wagons loaded with coffins too.

"Let's head to Fanny's. We'll hear the news. Then I'll take you home," Fargo said.

"Father is probably beside himself with worry," Laurel agreed.

Fargo tethered the pinto outside of Fanny's and Laurel took the infant while Fargo lifted the little girl and placed her on his shoulder. The boy slid down by himself and held Laurel's hand.

The five of them pushed through the front doors of Fanny's. The room was crowded with yammering citizens, each telling stories about the night's adventures and tragedies.

Then he heard a woman's desperate cry—"Alice! Charlie! Bobby!" and a young woman with sorrow-bruised eyes pushed forward, enfolding the children in her arms and sobbing with relief, followed by a man with a strained face and a torn shirt who picked up the boy and held him close.

Fargo and Laurel moved aside and suddenly Paul Cavendish was beside them, his arms around Laurel, kissing her hair.

"The Mortons have been frantic with worry," he said. "Their home was right on the bank and was swept away. The last they saw of the children, they were floating away on top of the front door."

"We found them a few miles downstream on a sandbar," Fargo said. "They have your daughter to thank for the baby's life."

"And you have Fargo to thank for my life," she said. Fargo saw the sudden exhaustion in her pale, drawn face.

"Why don't you get home for some rest," he suggested. She nodded agreement, kissed her father good-bye and then, suddenly, kissed Fargo on the cheek as well and left quickly.

"My daughter seems to have become very fond of you," Cavendish observed. Fargo could not quite read his tone.

"She's a fine young woman," Fargo said. "Independent and smart."

"Laurel knows her own mind," Cavendish said, fumbling in his coat pocket for a cigar. "She's the kind of woman who is going to do what she wants to do. No matter what the likes of you or I say."

"Agreed," Fargo said. And he knew the two of them had a perfect understanding about Laurel. Whatever she did was up to her.

"How about breakfast and a talk about business?" Cavendish said, motioning toward a table secluded in the back. "Are you up for that?"

"Sure," Fargo said, taking a seat.

"Got a special today," Fanny said, setting down two cups of coffee before them. "Cherry Creek mutton, all you can eat and then some."

"Is it fresh mutton?" Fargo asked, thinking of the sheep washed down with the flood.

"I guarantee it was on the hoof just last night," Fanny said with a wink.

"Sold," Fargo said.

"Make that two," Paul said.

As she moved away, Cavendish bent close to Fargo.

"Wyatt Roundtree and the decoy team left this morning, despite all the chaos," he said quietly. "A lot of folks were out on the streets cleaning up as they left, so the word is out about their departure. The question is, what's the best time for you and Sam to leave town?"

Fargo thought for a minute. He felt torn. On one hand, he was eager to get a move on with the gold shipment, eager to face the conspirators, if they found him on the trail. On the other hand, he thought of spending a few days in Denver City and finding time to be with Laurel. He imagined lingering for the rest of the week with her, perhaps riding out together onto the prairie.

But as he imagined that, he felt the nagging sense of danger, the pull of confusion about this gold shipment, about Cavendish, and about Booth. The more time passed and the farther away the decoy team got from Denver City, the more danger he would face on the trail.

"In order to do the best job for you," Fargo said at last, "I have to set out tomorrow. The sooner the better. Every day's delay will jeopardize our chances of success."

"I thought so as well," Cavendish agreed, "but I wanted your opinion. Tomorrow it is."

They ate the hearty breakfasts and Cavendish offered Fargo a cigar. They were just settling back to light them, their boots on the table, when Fargo heard screams outside the saloon.

"What now?" Cavendish muttered wearily. "Hasn't this town seen enough excitement?"

A man in overalls burst into the saloon, his face ashen.

"Indians! Indians uprising! We're all going to be slaughtered!"

There was instant pandemonium in the saloon as everyone stood, the men drawing their guns and the women crying out. Fargo tasted the panic in the air as he rose slowly to his feet. It would be bad for Fanny's business if he were to kill the upstairs guests by shooting through the ceiling, he reasoned, as he drew his Colt and plugged the floor three times.

The place quieted instantly and Fargo hopped up on a chair.

"You!" he called out to the man in overalls at the door. "Have you seen the Indians attacking?"

"No, but . . ."

"Do you know for certain that there's an uprising?"

"No, but . . ."

"Then what have you seen?"

"Out on the street. It's Howard Gates and his wife. We found 'em this morning up near their homestead at Running Creek." A few people nodded, recognizing the names. "Their bodies are outside. It ain't a sight women folk outta see. The Indians done tore 'em up real bad."

The room erupted in shouts and cries. The men's faces were grim as they filed out of Fanny's.

The bodies were laid in the back of a cart and a crowd of silent men stood around them. Howard Gates lay next to his wife, one arm flung across her as if to protect her, even after death. Both scalps were gone, sliced off raggedly, the skulls showing in patches through the dried black blood and clumps of remaining tangled hair around the ears. The faces were indistinguishable, a mass of bludgeoned flesh and bones, only the mouths recognizable, the jaws hanging loose, open in horror. The man's shirt had been torn away, the chest bristling with arrows, a dark black stain between his legs where the genitals had been mutilated. The woman's throat was slit open and a portion of her ragged dress had been tucked around her, but Fargo saw the seeping dark stains at her chest and between her legs. They had died a gruesome death. Fargo had a hopeless wish that the arrows and the knife had come quickly, before the rest.

"It's the goddamn Arapaho," one man said in a low voice.

"They're planning to attack," said another. "That's why they've moved their women and children away."

"We gotta attack them before they attack us," someone else said and Fargo heard the crowd muttering assent.

"Hold on a minute," Fargo said to the first man who had spoken. "This doesn't look like Arapaho work to me. Where did Gates homestead?"

"Up north in the mountains, near Twin Sisters," someone answered.

"Why would Arapaho venture into the mountains to kill homesteaders? It's not their territory," Fargo reasoned. He heard the crowd rumble uncomfortably.

"This was found under one of the bodies," a man said, stepping forward and offering a crumpled leather object to Fargo.

Fargo took it in his hands. The blood-soaked leather had dried and he forced it apart, unfolding it until he realized it was a mocassin. He examined the tattered beadwork on the instep, noting the distinctive U-shape pattern.

"Crow," he said. "Not Arapaho."

"Why are Crow wandering so far south?" Cavendish asked evenly. Fargo admired Paul's control of his voice and his thoughts, in marked contrast to the hot-headed men around them.

"Foraging. Exploring. Who knows?" Fargo mused, turning the mocassin over in his hands. "It was probably a small band of them. Gates probably put up a fight. Those Crow are halfway back to Dakota Territory by now. They won't attack a settlement as large as Denver City."

"Bullshit," one of the men said. "I don't care what you say, mocassin or no mocassin. This is the goddamn Arapaho and I say we attack!"

"What if it's n-n-not Arapaho? I-I-It's Indians just the same," a high voice said, and Fargo recognized the terrified stutter of Maximus Sweedler.

"I say let's go get us some Indian flesh!" another man shouted.

The crowd erupted in hot anger, fear fueling their passions and all about him Fargo heard men's frightened voices vowing to mutilate the Arapaho—women too—as their own had been.

Fargo thought of the Arapaho tribe he had seen crossing the wide valley, the women and children dragging the travois across the plains, the tall bronzed warriors riding in front. He felt the truth of what he had seen and what he knew—the Arapaho had gone from the banks of Cherry Creek to escape the coming flood.

"Let's say, for a moment, it is the Arapaho," Fargo said then, tossing the mocassin into the cart. He would have to try another strategy to avert what was sure to be a slaughter and possibly the start of a full-scale Indian war. The men fell silent at Fargo's unexpected concession.

"If it is the Arapaho, then this is just a trick to get us to attack them," Fargo said. There was silence as the men pondered this.

"That's right," a man added slowly. "That's how them Indians think."

"If we rode out to fight, they would have the advantage," Fargo added. "But, if we wait here and arm the city, we could drive them off if they attack."

"Yeah," another said. "We can get our guns together. Hole up in the center of town. Then just let those redskins attack us!"

"What if they set fire to the buildings?" another man asked.

"At least we'll have our lives," someone answered and Fargo recognized the gritty determination of the true pioneer.

"Tonight, we should mount a guard around the center of town. Put the women and children in the largest brick building," Fargo suggested.

"The mint," Cavendish offered.

"Yes, women, into the m-m-mint! All the w-w-women into the mint," a high quavering voice said in excitement.

Fargo recognized Sweedler's voice again, which was then lost in the rising babble. He caught Cavendish's eye and they withdrew from the crowd.

"You don't really believe there'll be an Indian attack tonight, do you?" Paul asked.

"No chance," Fargo said.

"Then what's the point of arming the town?"

"Gives them something to do, something to burn up the

anger and fear. By tomorrow, they'll calm down and forget about going after the Arapaho.''

"Then, you just saved a lot of lives,'' Cavendish said. "White and Indian.''

"Let's hope so,'' Fargo said. "Meanwhile, let's get this organized.''

The late afternoon sun poured molten gold over the dusty streets as they walked westward. They passed groups of men hurrying to their stations, rifles in hand, strapped with belts of extra ammunition. The ten block area in the center of Denver City had been staked out. Men had pulled wagons into the streets around the perimeter and had taken up posts behind them for the long night's watch.

The brick building of the mint loomed ahead of them, its wide doors open. The afternoon breeze fluttered the skirts of the women as they stood about in knots, talking excitedly, their children running and tumbling in the dust.

Coming toward them down the street were two familiar figures, pulling a painted cart. Cavendish saw them too and groaned.

"I suppose Sweedler will have a captive audience tonight,'' Paul commented, nodding toward the cart.

"That's one way of looking at it,'' Fargo said, watching the strange pair as they approached the doorway and shooed several of the women aside. Wilhelmina Sweedler was coughing, over and over, a dry hacking. "Look, they're planning to pull that thing inside the mint.'' He and Cavendish started forward.

"Leave it outside, Sweedler,'' Cavendish said, approaching them. Wilhelmina Sweedler whirled at the sound of his voice, her face betraying sudden panic, the nostrils of her sharp nose flaring.

"These remedies are priceless,'' she protested.

"T-T-That's right,'' Maximus agreed, his head bobbing up and down. "P-P-Priceless.''

Cavendish threw up his hands. "Alright,'' he said. He and Fargo watched as the two pushed the cart easily up the two steps to the boardwalk and through the wide doors, over the threshold. They followed them inside. The main room of the mint was crowded with bedrolls, cots, picnic baskets, and bodies. Wilhelmina and Maximus wheeled the cart across the room and parked it next to the door leading to Cavendish's office. Sweedler had already raised the flap of the cart.

"Come on, Sweedler," Cavendish called out. "The mint's not for the menfolk tonight. Let's go."

Fargo expected a windy protest from Maximus, but instead, the pudgy green-suited man simply shrugged, bid his wife good-bye and left. She had another loud attack of coughing just after he left.

"Well, I'm glad he's not staying," Laurel said, coming up to stand beside them. "I thought for a moment we'd have to listen to his sales pitch all night long."

"No, but you will have to listen to Mrs. Sweedler coughing," Fargo said. "She can't seem to stop."

"I'll go see if I can help her," Laurel said, moving away.

"I'll be moving out," Fargo said.

Cavendish looked at him questioningly.

"Moving out?" he asked.

"I'm scouting the plains tonight. See where the Arapaho are. See what's lurking around, if anything," Fargo answered.

"I'll let the others know after you've gone," Cavendish said.

"Good," Fargo said, his eyes following Laurel's graceful form as she made her way across the room. "I'll see you along about morning, if all goes well."

To his right, the evening star flickered above the range, a silver burning against the diminishing pale blue band of the day gone by. To the east, black velvet night ascended the sky dome, where only stars gave out their pale luminescence. There would be no moon tonight, Fargo thought with satisfaction. The wide bowl of Denver City was far behind as the Trailsman rode due south, following the track left by the Arapaho tribe.

His pinto moved through the tall buffalo grass as quietly as the stir of breeze, with no saddle to creak, no reins to flap, no bridle to clink in the airy stillness. Fargo rode bareback, guiding the Ovaro with his knees, the palms of his hands on the horse's neck. He wore dark jeans and his chest was bare, smeared, along with his face and hands, with the black odorless silt from the creek. Strapped to one leg was the throwing knife.

After several hours, the faint smell of woodsmoke entered his keen nostrils and he quietly laid a hand on the horse's neck. It halted. Fargo sat up straight, turning his head from side to side slowly, inhaling the cool air to determine the distance and direction of the Indian camp.

He was downwind, which was to his advantage. The fire would be a mile ahead at least. He spotted a stand of cottonwoods, a dark mound against the pale grasses with a distinctive notch, which he memorized for his return. He guided the Ovaro toward it and, in the darkness underneath, slid silently down. The pinto would remain until he returned. He set off, walking through the buffalo grass, the faint silvery swish of his passing heard only by the wind.

He saw the first guard silhouetted against the stars, a solitary figure which loomed suddenly on a ridge before him. Fargo dropped slowly to his knees, grateful for the cover of the sage stand along which he was creeping. He crouched still, waiting long moments, watching until the stars reappeared. He waited a long time more and then crawled forward again.

He did not see, but he heard the second guard. The two notes like those of the burrowing owl came out of the silence behind him as he crawled through the grass. But it was not an owl. He continued his careful progress, wondering if the call signified safety or an alarm. He would know soon, he thought.

The smell of burning greasewood intensified and then mixed with the rich odors of roasted meat, tanned leather, horse manure, cooking herbs, and the warm and familiar human smell.

Fargo was moving inch by inch now, through a scraggly stand of rabbit bush, belly to the ground, sliding himself over the roots and under the low branches. On the leaves above him, he saw a dull red glow and he raised himself slowly to peer over the hillock before him and into the Arapaho camp.

The broad cones of the teepees were lit, here and there, by the dying red campfires. The braves sat in a circle, their faces golden in the firelight, listening to the chant of an old man in a wide yellow headband whose hands were carving the air in front of him as he sang. Behind the old man was a teepee painted with decorative circles around the top and horizontal stripes girding the middle. Fargo listened. He was close enough to hear the pop of the fire and to distinguish the Algonquian words. He strained to hear sentences he could translate, fearing words of strategy, plans for war.

First he caught the term for the evening star and then the words for mating, father, ancestors. He watched as the old man raised his hands above his head and described a great circle. "The beginning of time," he heard the old man say. Fargo smiled to himself. The braves had gathered in the darkness to hear their oldest story. This was no plan for attack. He silently backed out of the rabbit bush and retraced his steps under the star-studded night.

6

The first light of dawn swept down the mountains and washed the plains, slowly filling the distant wide bowl on the bottom of which Denver City lay like a shower of dark pebbles. Fargo clucked to the pinto and galloped downward toward the town. The outskirts were deserted, the citizens still holed up in the center of town waiting for the Indian attack. He turned the corner of a city street and approached the barricade. From a distance, he could see moving figures of men behind the wagons they had pulled across the dusty streets.

A rifle cracked ahead of him and a shot whizzed over his head. He had forgotten the black smears of silt and his strange appearance. He was unrecognizable. The shot had been a warning, aimed high. The second would not be.

"Hey!" he yelled, reining in and waving at the narrow-eyed faces and rifle barrels which protruded over the edges of the wagons. "It's me—Skye Fargo!"

The rifles lowered uncertainly, until he heard a voice say "Damned if it ain't. What are you doing in that getup? 'Bout got your head blowed off." A skinny man in a checked shirt stood up scratching his neck and peering at Fargo as he rode forward.

"I was spying on the Arapaho camp," Fargo answered as he drew near.

"We heard you'd gone. But we figured you were just scared. We figured you just wanted to ride in the other direction," a brown-bearded man said as he stepped forward.

"Nope," Fargo said slowly, dismounting. "I thought somebody ought to look around. I found the Arapaho in camp, half a day's ride south. Peaceful as jackrabbits. We'll have no trouble from them."

"We're going to have trouble from those savages or my name ain't Budge Hays," the brown-bearded man said, peering at Skye suspiciously. "Seems to me those Indians can get stirred up over nothing. We ought to teach 'em a lesson right now. While we still can.''

"From what I saw last night, you'd be going after the wrong Indians," Fargo said.

"Redskins is redskins," he heard another man mutter. "They're all alike."

"Besides," Budge Hays continued, "the Indians only respect killing. I say hit 'em. Hit 'em hard."

Fargo heard murmurs of approval. He was too tired to argue with Budge Hays and the rest of them. The men were still shaken from the flood, and from the sight of the mutilated bodies of Gates and his wife. In a day or two, they would settle down. He hoped. But this Budge Hays, he wouldn't settle down so easily. He'd seen the type before. Big mouth. Big trouble.

Fargo shook his head and said nothing more. He led his horse around the barricade into the center of town. As he passed the mint, the doors opened. Several women emerged, one of them Laurel. She spotted him and gave a cry, running across the street, to throw her arms about him.

"Father told me you'd gone!" she said. "I'm so glad you're back safely."

"Whoa," he said, holding her at arm's length and looking at the black silt smearing her face and dress.

"You do look a sight," she said.

"So do you," he answered.

She looked down at her front and laughed.

"What did you find out there?" she asked him, suddenly serious and attentive.

Fargo thought for a moment. How to explain the night?

"Stars. Grass. Owls. And a camp of quiet Indians," he said at last.

"Sounds beautiful," she said.

They heard a commotion and turned to see the Sweedlers trying to drag their painted cart out of the front doors of the mint. It had become stuck on the threshold, and three men were helping to push it without much luck. The wooden wheels of the cart groaned and then came free, lumbering across the boardwalk and jouncing heavily down the two short steps. The Sweedlers seemed in a hurry as they hastily thanked the men for helping them and then pushed the cumbersome cart slowly down the street.

Fargo watched the Sweedlers and something tugged at his memory. Something was amiss, something that didn't fit. He tried to pin it down for a moment, but it swam away. He felt the weariness fall on him like a heavy blanket, weariness from the events of the last two days—the flood, the massacre and hysteria, the preparations for the supposed Indian attack, the long night of wakefulness, riding and scouting. He knew he needed a few hours rest. By early afternoon, he thought, it would be time to ride out with Sam.

"Fargo!"

They turned to see Paul Cavendish approaching.

"What did you find out there? Are the Arapaho on the warpath?" he asked.

"Not a chance," Fargo answered.

"That's a relief," Cavendish said. "And how was your night in the mint, Laurel?" he asked, putting an arm around his daughter.

"Fine," she answered. "Except Mrs. Sweedler kept us up most of the night with her coughing, until . . ."

"You mean she didn't try to sell you anything?" Cavendish cut in with a chuckle.

"Not a thing," Laurel said. "She just kept coughing and apologizing that she was keeping everybody up."

"Too bad," Cavendish muttered distractedly. "Let's go inside, Skye. We need to talk over a few details."

"I'm sure you didn't stop for breakfast yet, Father," Laurel said, plucking at his sleeve. "You either, Skye. I'll pack a basket and bring it to the mint."

"If you run into Sam, send him over," said Paul.

Fargo watched her slim figure move lightly up the dusty street, her hair blowing behind her like golden waves in the early morning breeze. She waved to several of the townspeople as she walked along.

"She's settled into Denver City very quickly," Fargo said.

"Laurel's a friendly girl. And strong willed," Cavendish said. "Just like her mother." Fargo heard the note of wistfulness in his voice. "Let's get going," he said quickly, in a businesslike voice.

Just then they heard a woman's scream. A horse and rider galloped wildly down the street scattering the townspeople

98

before him. A small boy was chasing a puppy in the dusty street, oblivious to the oncoming horse. Fargo started forward, measuring the distance between himself and the child and the galloping rider. He would not get there in time. At the last moment, the rider reined in, the horse reared, his hooves coming down near the boy who jumped up and ran away. The rider was Booth.

A skinny man in overalls came running up the block.

"You almost killed my kid!" he exclaimed to Booth, who sat sullenly on his horse.

"Teach him not to play in the street."

"Now, wait just a minute, mister," the man retorted.

The watching crowd murmured.

"You wanna make something of it?" Booth said, dropping his hand to his holster.

"Well . . ." the skinny man said slowly. "I guess not."

"Whaddya mean, not making something of it?" a voice from the crowd said. "That could have been any one of us. There's laws in this town about being reckless." This had gone too far, Fargo thought. Just then, the crowd parted and the sheriff pushed his way through.

"What's going on here?"

"This man almost ran down my kid," the skinny man said, pointing at Booth. The crowd muttered assent.

"Look, Booth," the sheriff said, his thick black brows lowered. "I've had six complaints about you in the last week. That's six too many. I'm dang tired of your shenanigans. You got a choice. You cool yourself off in my jailhouse for a week or you get out of town for a month. Starting now. Take your pick."

Booth's eyes flashed and his grip tightened on his pistol. A long moment passed and then he holstered it.

"I'll get out," he said. He put his spurs to his horse and galloped up the street.

"What makes him tick?" Fargo asked, shaking his head as he walked with Paul toward the mint.

"Strange fellow, isn't he?" Paul said. "Ever since he was fired from the mint, he's been a bitter man."

"Why doesn't he get away from Denver City? Start over someplace else?" Fargo asked.

"Everybody wonders that," Cavendish replied. "He's

hanging around here for something. Probably no good. I just try to stay out of his way.''

They entered the main door of the mint. The front room was still crowded with women folding blankets and their menfolk helping them carry out the heavy baskets and folding cots. Cavendish greeted some of them as they wended their way through the room toward his office door. He drew a key from his pocket and inserted it into the lock. He gave it a half turn and a puzzled look came over his face. The door swung open.

"That's strange," he said under his breath. "I could have sworn I had locked this door last night before we opened the mint for the townspeople."

He paused, turned the key left and right again, finally withdrawing it.

"Curious," he said quietly. "Come inside."

As Skye seated himself, Cavendish approached the huge wall safe behind his desk. Paul bent over to look carefully at the setting on the dial. Then he pulled down on the handle. It didn't budge.

"Hmmm . . ." he said.

He walked about the room, tugging at the wooden file drawers which lined the room, but all of them were locked. He did the same with the desk drawers.

"Must have forgotten to lock my office door last night. In all the excitement," Cavendish said, his brow still lowered. "Well, let's talk."

They heard a knock at the door and Sam entered.

"You called, boss?"

"Come on in and sit down," Paul said, gesturing toward a chair.

"So, what's the plan?" Fargo asked.

"I've closed the mint for four days, until Monday morning. I told all the employees to help get the city cleaned up from the flood. By this afternoon, the mint will be deserted. I'll come back here in midafternoon and load the gold ingots into wooden crates. At three o'clock, drive your wagon down the alleyway in back. I'll let you in the rear gate to the loading yard. It's protected from the street and no one can see us there. We'll load the crates into the bottom of your wagon, underneath all the other gear. Then you're away. If anyone sees you leaving town, it will look like you're off to pan gold."

"Sounds simple enough," Fargo said.

They heard another knock at the door and Laurel's voice.

"Come in," Cavendish said.

She entered, carrying a basket and a tin pot of coffee.

"I ate already. I'll skedaddle," said Sam. "All this talk about hitting the trail has put me in the mood for some mule buying. I'm going over to the stable again to haggle. I bet I can get the price down on Bessietoo. We're going to need a smart mule to lead the team."

Sam left and Laurel unpacked fragrant biscuits and three tin mugs. Fargo wiped his hands on his Levi's, but only some of the silt came off. He took a biscuit anyway.

"Exactly how much gold are we hauling?" Fargo asked as he took a bite of warm bread.

"Almost half a ton," said Cavendish. "Our ingots are one thousand ounces of pure Colorado Territory gold. That's about sixty-two pounds, worth $2,000 a bar. You'll be carrying fifteen ingots, packed three to a case."

"Makes $30,000 in gold, total," Fargo said. "That's an attractive package for a band of conspirators."

He saw Laurel shiver as she took another sip of coffee.

"What does $30,000 worth of gold look like?" she said. "Is it here?"

"In the safe," Cavendish answered. "Would you like to see it before Mr. Fargo hauls it east?"

She nodded.

Cavendish turned to the safe, carefully standing between them and the dial so that neither of them could read the combination numbers. Fargo's acute hearing caught the faint sound of the clicking of cogs as Paul dialed the combination. Then there was a low thunk as the mechanism fell into place. Cavendish took a step backward, grasping the heavy bar and pulling it downward as he swung the large safe door open.

Inside the safe were three broad shelves. On the top one, Fargo saw some currency bound in neat bundles, leather bags, with drawstrings, and piles of golden coins in several different sizes and thicknesses. The second shelf held the ingots, stacked three high and five deep, gleaming gold in the semidarkness inside the safe. Each shining bar was stamped "Auraria Private Mint" along the side, the letters molded deep into the soft yellow gold.

"Goddamn it . . ." Cavendish said, standing stock still and looking into the safe.

Fargo glanced at Paul's face which was reddening, and followed his gaze. Cavendish was staring in disbelief at the bottom shelf which held several folded canvas bags, all empty.

"Father! What's the matter?" Laurel asked, jumping up from her chair and walking around the desk to stand beside him. "The ingots are there. Whatever is wrong?"

Cavendish seemed to have lost his voice. He rubbed his eyes and looked again into the safe.

"It's the gold dust. It's gone."

"What?" Laurel asked.

"I kept it in these canvas bags. We collect a quantity of it and then melt and refine it. There was over $25,000 worth," he said. "But how can it be gone? This is a new safe. It's always locked. It can't be cracked. At least that's what they said when I bought it."

"Anybody else know the combination?" Fargo asked.

"No," Cavendish said. Just then he heard a knock at the office door.

"Say nothing about this," Cavendish whispered, quickly pushing the safe door shut behind him, but not locking it. "Come in!"

The door opened and Fanny entered, her round face all smiles as she saw Fargo and Laurel. Then she caught sight of Paul's face.

"What's wrong, Paul?" Fanny asked.

"See for yourself," Cavendish said, easing the door open again. "Gold dust. Twenty-five grand. Gone."

"Out of the safe?" Fanny exclaimed. "Now why ever would somebody take gold dust and not the bars? Or the cash and the coins?"

"Easier to hide," Paul suggested. "Impossible to trace. Not stamped Auraria Private Mint."

"When was the last time you saw the gold dust in the safe?" Fargo asked Paul.

"Day before yesterday," he answered slowly, thinking back. "Before the flood. At the end of the business day, I added some gold dust to one of the bags, exchanging it for some currency. That night was the party. And then the flood."

"Does Matthew Booth know the combination to this safe?" Fargo asked.

Cavendish shot him a sharp look.

"Yes," he said thoughtfully. "Matthew Booth would be a likely suspect. But, in answer to your question, no. No, Booth does not know the combination. I ordered this new safe myself. It arrived long after Booth was gone from the mint."

"Then it had to have happened last night, when the women and children were in the mint," Fargo said. "Laurel, why don't you tell us what happened in here last night?"

"Well, of course it was very crowded. Most of the women bedded down early. Except for Wilhelmina . . . except for Wilhelmina Sweedler." Suspicion crossed Laurel's face like a cloud. "Of course! How could I have been so stupid? Her words began to tumble out of her, faster and faster. "She was coughing and coughing. She kept apologizing for keeping us up. But there was something about her cough that didn't sound right."

"Like she was faking it," said Fargo.

"Exactly!" Laurel said. "Late in the night, I went to fetch some water for one of the women. When I got back, Mrs. Sweedler had moved herself and the cart into Father's office."

"What?" Cavendish said. "But I locked the door."

Laurel paused.

"Go on," Fargo said.

"I looked in on her and she was lying on a blanket on the floor. She woke up a little and said she had moved inside so that her coughing wouldn't keep the rest of us up all night!"

"But how did she get into the safe?" Cavendish wondered.

"The same way she got into your office," Fargo said. "With her handy tool kit, and those long sensitive fingers. Remember how easily she fixed your pocket watch?"

"And my grandfather clock!" Fanny interjected. "Why that weasel!"

"Exactly," Fargo agreed.

"How could I have been so stupid?" Laurel wailed. She rose and went to Paul. "Father, I'm so sorry. I just assumed your office door was unlocked."

"And who would guess she would pick open the safe? You were tired, Laurel. It was the middle of the night," he said, putting his arms around her. "It's not your fault."

"It also explains why she didn't take the ingots. She couldn't. They were too heavy," Fargo observed.

"So, she took the gold dust," said Fanny angrily, "bit by bit. Put it into that damn cart of theirs! And they checked out of my hotel this morning."

"Any idea where they were heading?" Fargo asked.

"Not a clue," Fanny said. "Ooooooh, if I'd only known!" she added, shaking her round fist.

They were all quiet for a few moments. Fargo remembered watching the Sweedlers pushing the heavy cart over the threshold that morning. Something hadn't seemed right about it. And now he knew what it was. He remembered seeing them the day before, rolling the cart into the mint, and how easily the light cart had bounced over the threshold. That was what had been bothering him. If only he had made the connection and stopped them. Now he wondered how far they had gotten. And which direction they had gone.

"Let's call the sheriff," Laurel suggested. "He'll get a posse together and go after them."

"I don't think I can risk that," Cavendish said.

"Risk? What risk?" Fanny asked.

"The investors," Cavendish said. "That gold dust is almost a whole year's profit. If the investors know it's missing, we'll have a run on the stock. They'll be storming the mint, wanting their money back. That could be a disaster for business."

"Then what?" Laurel asked.

Cavendish looked up at Fargo. "Maybe we could get the gold back . . . quietly," he said.

"I thought that might be coming," Fargo said. "But what about the . . . " He glanced at Fanny.

"The gold shipment," Cavendish said. "Fanny knows about that. The shipment will just have to wait."

"But if the conspirators get to the decoy team and find out they don't have the gold—" Fargo said.

"They'll head back here," Cavendish added. "Let's hope by then the gold dust will be back in the safe, the Sweedlers will be locked up, and you'll be long gone, heading east."

"Leaving no trail," Fargo said.

"So, the Sweedlers. How much?" Cavendish asked.

"They won't be too hard to catch. I can hear Maximus a mile away," Fargo said. "Make it an extra $500."

"Sold," Cavendish said. "Here it is. In advance." He tossed a short stack of bills toward Fargo.

"I'd better get going," Fargo said, stashing the money inside his shirt. "I don't want to be setting out with the gold shipment about the time those conspirators arrive back in Denver City. Thanks for breakfast."

He nodded to Fanny and Laurel.

"Good luck," Laurel said.

As he was leaving, he saw Cavendish close the door of the safe and twirl the dial once, twice, three times, before he turned back to the desk.

Fargo walked out into the bright sunshine. Several passers-by eyed him suspiciously and he remembered the silt which still clung to him, head to foot. He spotted a drinking trough and headed toward it, bending down to pump the crystal clear cold water over his head and neck. A real bath would have to wait. He continued up the street, enjoying the morning air on his wet face.

Now for the Sweedlers, he thought. There was nothing to be learned at the hotel. Maybe the stable owner would have some answers.

When he arrived, he heard Sam's excited voice.

"How could you sell her?"

"Man met my price," the stable owner said stoutly.

Fargo walked into the stable yard. Sam sighted him.

"Fargo! You'll never guess who . . ."

"In a minute, Sam," Fargo said darkly. Sam fell silent, catching on that something serious was afoot. "Could you bring my horse around?" he asked the man. "Saddled?" That would take him a few moments, Fargo thought. He didn't want to tell Sam about the missing gold dust in front of anyone.

As soon as the stable owner dissappeared into the stalls, Sam drew close to Fargo.

"Just let me tell you what's up here," Sam sputtered, his gray beard shaking with excitement.

"Let me guess," Fargo said. "Sweedler bought Bessie-too."

Sam's mouth gaped.

"And he's left town," Fargo added.

"Now how would you just guess a durn thing like that?" Sam asked. "That's exactly it! Oh, I was a fool not to buy that mule when I had a chance. And I hate the idea of her under the whip of that old snake-oil sleaze. But hey. Where are you off to?"

"I'm going after the Sweedlers," Fargo said, and he told Sam about the missing gold. "So, I guess Sweedler bought the mule to help haul the extra weight."

"Count me in," Sam said.

"Now, Sam . . ."

"No, Fargo. Durn it. You go after that Sweedler fellow, and I'll go after Bessietoo. It's my own fault for not buying her when I could."

The Ovaro was being led from the stables, saddled and ready.

"But what are you going to ride, Sam?"

"Oh, hell," Sam muttered. "Just when I don't have a good mule. Wait here. I could run back to Fanny's, grab my cash, get a mule and come along!"

"No time for that," Fargo said. "And we've got to make good time. No mules. Let's get you a decent horse." He pulled the wad of cash out of his shirt.

"If I buy a horse from you this morning, can I sell it back to you later today?" he asked the stable owner.

"Well," the man said, rubbing his unshaven chin. "Lemme see. The horse will be a bit used up, I imagine . . ."

"And probably not worth as much," Fargo added.

"Oh, this is ridiculous," Sam cut in. "Let's get a mule. A mule holds his value."

"I suppose I'd buy it back," said the man. "But you'd take a loss. Maybe ten percent?"

"Let me see what you've got for sale," Fargo said. "Something fast, but not too rough."

The stable owner showed them four horses and Sam chose a bay, gentle but with good legs. The saddle, bridle and blanket came along with the horse. Fargo peeled off several large bills and handed them over as Sam mounted with a groan.

Fargo swung himself into his saddle and the pinto whinnied, eager to be away. Fargo turned back.

"You don't happen to know which way that fast-talking fellow went?" he asked.

"That fat one who bought the mule from me this morning?" the man said, looking up at Fargo and squinting in the sun. "Don't reckon so."

They were about to ride out of the yard, when the man turned back. "Hey, wait a minute," he called. "He had some woman with him. Kind of dark, skinny like a shadow. Now she did ask me how far it was to Kansas City. Does that help you?"

"Might," Fargo said. "Thanks."

"Hot diggety!" Sam said as they rode out of the stableyard. "We even know where they're heading."

"Don't be too sure of that," Fargo said.

They rode up the street, keeping the horses to a sedate trot. No need to draw undue attention. As they approached the city limits, they took the eastward trail.

They rode hard under the hot sun, the miles passing beneath them. Fargo kept a sharp eye on the trail ahead, his hope falling as two hours passed. The Sweedlers had a headstart of a couple of hours. They should have caught up to them by now.

She was clever, Mrs. Wilhelmina Sweedler, he thought. She must have figured that they would head to the stable owner to ask him questions. Did she ask about Kansas City to throw them off the trail? Then where were they really heading? If he were the Sweedlers, he thought, he would make for Cheyenne. It was a fast journey. And from there, they could travel north to join the swarm of settlers going west on the Oregon Trail.

Fargo reined in and Sam halted.

"They're not this way," he said. "We'll have to backtrack and try the trail northward to Cheyenne."

"Lead on," Sam said.

When they reached the crossing of the trails, they turned onto the trail to Cheyenne, which led north from Denver City on almost a straight line, interrupted only by the fords at Little

Thompson, Big Thompson, and Cache La Poudre rivers. Fargo took the lead and set an easy pace. He glanced back from time to time to check on Sam, who jounced along on his bay, clutching the reins. Sam was having a hard time keeping his seat. He was used to the steady loping, slower rhythm of mules.

It was another in the string of clear spring days, the deep blue sky overhead uninterrupted by clouds. He caught a flash of yellow in a stand of sage and heard the flutelike call of the meadowlark, and saw the bird's yellow and black throat pulse with the sound. The land began to roll under them, as if a giant hand had pushed the folds of a blanket and plucked up a few cone-shaped hills which pierced the bright horizon and then fell away behind them as they moved steadily northward. They rode down into the broad valley of the Little Thompson, where the shadbushes grew thick.

The Little Thompson was high, but they forded easily, climbing the trail upward again, out of the valley. The northern plain spread out wide before them. Fargo reined in and scanned the horizon. Ahead of them, the trail rose and fell on the long rises. In the far distance, he thought he saw a movement, some dark shape on the trail. He wondered if it could be the Sweedlers.

Then he heard a low throbbing, barely audible, as if a thousand Indian drums were beating. The sound vibrated through the earth. The pinto shifted nervously under him.

"Skye. What's that?" Sam asked, drawing up behind him.

"Shhhh."

Fargo listened. The vibration grew in intensity, yet all seemed still around him. Even the birds creased singing. He could see nothing moving. He turned his head from side to side, trying to locate the direction of the sound. The vibration increased, and he realized—

"Ride!" he shouted to Sam, spurring his horse. "Stampede!"

7

The horses leapt forward, catching panic from the increasing sound. The ground flew away beneath them and the brush was a blur as they galloped up the trail.

Fargo turned to look behind. The sun-bright crest of the hill was suddenly a dark line. Then the hillside blackened slowly, as if molasses were pouring over it, running in rivulets down the side and filling the vale. Thousands of head of buffalo pounded over the hill behind them in a mad dash that had no destination. And Sam and Fargo were directly in their path.

As their horses galloped, Fargo looked back again to measure the width of the herd. If they pulled their mounts to the west of the trail, they would be alongside the stampede and safe. Maybe. He turned in his saddle again and looked forward. Something else caught his eye.

Their breathless gallop to stay in front of the buffalo stampede had already brought them several miles northward. Fargo saw again the dark shape on the trail ahead of them. Now they were near enough to make it out. It looked like a caterpillar crawling down the side of a slope—a wagon train, headed due south, directly into the path of the stampede.

Skye had seen wagons and even homesteads caught in stampedes and it wasn't a pretty sight. Stampeding buffalo were crazed, too panicked to turn aside. They would trample anything in their path—wagons, horses, settlers. He glanced over at Sam, who clung, ashen faced, to the back of his bay.

Fargo pointed forward toward the wagon train. Sam squinted his eyes and then nodded to Fargo. He had seen. Fargo cocked his head over toward the east. Sam nodded, and they reined their horses off the trail and across the prairie.

Fargo hoped neither of their mounts would step in a prairie-dog hole and break a leg.

Their diagonal course cut across the path of the oncoming herd, slowing them. The buffalo drew nearer; the pounding of their hooves grew louder. Fargo let the Ovaro have his lead, trusting the sturdy horse to choose the best footing through the brush. He looked again toward the wagon train in the distance and back toward the herd. If nothing went wrong, they would just make it and have enough time to turn the stampede.

As they drew even with the western edge of the running buffalo, Fargo drew his Colt revolver and saw Sam draw his rifle. With a nod, both of them turned in their saddles and fired. One buffalo fell. The buffalo around the fallen one ran on, turning only slightly. Fargo shot five times more into the herd, bringing down a buffalo calf, but they ran on. Sam looked at Skye with fear in his eyes. The wagon train was nearer. Fargo could see figures running around it, in panic at the approaching danger.

They'd have to get in good and close to turn the herd. Fargo reined in the pinto, which resisted, wanting to stay well out in front of the thundering buffalo. But finally, the horse fell back until they galloped just a stride in front of the herd.

Fargo took off his hat and held it in one hand. Waving it over his head and fluttering it toward the ground, he yelled as he rode. The bison nearest him shied away, jostling others which turned eastward. Sam joined him, mimicking his actions and the buffalo began to turn, more and more of them.

Fargo shouted until his throat hurt, and waved his hat again and again, turning more of the buffalo. He slowed the pinto even more until they galloped in the front line of the stampede. The buffalo brushed up against the Ovaro, and he saw their dark thick brows and stubby horns, their magnificent shoulders and the pale gold tufted fur on their backs. He continued to shout and wave, concentrating only on the herd as they turned gradually.

When he looked up again, he saw that they now rode on a northeast line, at the flank of the stampede, heading back out onto the open plains. The wagon train was a smear of color as Fargo and Sam dashed by whooping and waving their hats overhead.

A mile out onto the trail, Fargo reined in and Sam pulled up. They watched as the flank of the stampede passed by and the herd thundered out eastward, the sound dying away gradually.

"Don't tell me a mule could have done that!" Fargo said.

"Hell no," Sam said, breathless from the ride. "A good one would have just brayed. And skeered the living daylights out of those bison."

"Let's drop in on the wagon train," Fargo said.

They turned and rode back to the trail. The horses were drenched in sweat. The wagon train was still halted, the men with their rifles drawn, and anxiously watching them.

"Hey, strangers!" one of the men called out. "That was sure some fancy riding you did."

Fargo and Sam drew up and dismounted.

"We sure are grateful to you," another man said, stepping forward. "Name's Slade. Marcus Slade."

"I'm Fargo and this is my partner Sam."

"Hey mister!" Fargo felt a tug on his jacket and he looked down. A small towheaded boy looked up at him. "D'ye think them elephants will come back?"

"This here is my son, Quentin," Slade said, pulling the boy back.

"I think they're gone for good," Fargo answered.

"Shucks," the boy said.

"We're looking for a certain gentleman and his wife," Fargo said, pulling the brim of his hat down. "Wonder if you folks have met anybody on the trail?"

"Few miles back we ran into one of them salesmen. Heading the opposite way, going toward Wyoming."

Fargo nodded. "Patent medicines?"

"Yup. With the goddamndest . . ."

"Marcus!" a woman called out from the wagon.

" 'Scuse my language. I mean to say, the awfullest painted-up cart this side of Hades."

"Sounds like the people we're looking for," said Fargo.

"I bet they tried to sell you lots of ointments," Sam said.

"Now, that was the funny thing," said Slade. "We didn't

want any ointments, but my wife took it into her head that we needed some more salt. We've been running low. Wouldn't sell her none, though. Said 'salt' right there on the side of that cart. We called after them, but they never stopped. Funniest salesman I ever seen.''

"How long ago did you pass them?" Fargo asked.

"Oh, along about half an hour," Slade said.

"Thanks," Fargo said, swinging into his saddle.

"Nah, it's us who are mighty obliged to you," Slade said.

Fargo and Sam galloped north, following the descending trail into the valley of the Big Thompson River. As they mounted the crest of a rise, Fargo saw below them the wide water, glittering silver in the sun. Thickets of peachleaf willow outlined the curving edge of the river. On the near bank were the Sweedlers.

Fargo and Sam reined in and looked down. Eight mules were hitched to the Sweedlers' mountain wagon, and behind it was the painted cart. Maximus was having trouble with the mules. They were in revolt. They stood on the bank of the Big Thompson River, heels dug in, while Maximus walked back and forth alongside them. He drew his whip and cracked it over their heads, but there was no movement. Fargo knew what was coming and he saw the heavy whip descend on the nearest mule. It was too much for Sam and he yowled, putting the spur to his bay and galloping off down the hill toward the Sweedlers. Fargo followed.

Maximus looked up to see the two horses coming down the slope toward him. He jumped onto the mountain wagon and Fargo saw Wilhelmina grab the whip from her husband. She stood up on the driver's seat and lashed the mule team again and again.

After a moment, the team lurched forward, pulling the wagons into the wide stream, the rippling water rising around the animals' haunches. Halfway across, the mules stopped. They refused to budge, despite Wilhelmina's efforts with the whip.

Sam had arrived at the bank by then, followed closely by Fargo. The pinto and the bay plunged into the river, wading easily through the shallow water and drawing alongside the wagon. Mrs. Sweedler had given up on the mules and sat back down, tight-lipped.

Fargo tipped his hat to the Sweedlers.

"Maximus! Mrs. Sweedler! Fancy meeting you way out here," he said. "What's your hurry?"

"Wh-Wh-Why are you follow—" Maximus began. Wilhelmina glanced up at them and seemed to collect herself.

"Why, Mr. Fargo!" she interrupted. "Thank heavens it's you. We thought we were being chased by a couple of bandits!"

"Th-th-that's—"

"You could help us," she said. She smiled at Fargo, and he did not like the glitter in her dark eyes. "It seems we are stuck."

"You are," Fargo said.

The Ovaro shifted a few steps, gaining a steady foothold on the bottom of the riverbed. Fargo took a long look at the mountain wagon and the painted cart. The water reached to the hubs of the wheels. Sam eyed the Sweedlers with undisguised disdain.

"I guess we could help you some," Skye said slowly. "First we need to get these mules out of the stream. Sam, get these critters unhitched and over onto the bank."

"N-now, wait a min—minute!" Maximus protested.

"You want our help or not?" Fargo said.

The Sweedlers were grim, as they watched Sam lean over and unharness Bessietoo from the lead position. One by one, he unhitched all the mules and led them out of the traces and onto the bank, where he picketed them in a grassy area.

"But how are you going to get the wagon out of the river?" Mrs. Sweedler asked as the last of the mules was led away, leaving the two wagons sitting in the middle of the stream.

"We aren't," Fargo said.

"H-H-Hey! Th-th-this is unfair!" Maximus shouted, rising from the driver's seat, his face bright red. Sam remounted his bay and rode out again into the stream beside Fargo.

"At least not yet," Fargo said. "First I'd like to buy a few of your fine wares."

He guided the pinto alongside the painted cart and opened the side. The wooden prop fell down into place, holding up the lid. Inside were the rows of bottles, blue, pale green, yellow, and clear, suspended the leather loops which kept them from breaking on the rough trail. Fargo glanced along the bottom of the cart, measuring the inside with the outside. There was no false bottom here, he thought. Where had they stashed the gold dust?

"How about a bag of salt?" Sam suggested.

"Not for sale," Wilhelmina said.

"Strange . . . ." Fargo said, eyeing the bulging canvas bags of salt in the back of the mountain wagon.

"I mean . . . we have orders for this salt in Cheyenne. We can't sell it to you."

"Well, we could just wait here until you do have a bag for sale," Fargo said.

"You have no right to hold us here!" Wilhelmina said.

"We could . . . we could . . . ."

"Call the sheriff?" Sam suggested.

The Sweedlers sat stony faced.

"But if the salt was for sale," Fargo said thoughtfully, "how much do you reckon a whole bag would cost?"

"Fifty dollars for the bag," Maximus said. "Or . . . forty-five."

"Just to be fair," Fargo said, "I'll pay fifty. Wouldn't want to rob you." He reached into his shirt, withdrew the cash Paul Cavendish had given him and peeled off a bill.

"Not for sale!" Wilhelmina protested. "I tell you the salt is already spoken for."

"Now dear," Maximus said, patting her hand. "If we let him buy a bag, he'll let us go. Any bag of salt."

Fargo saw the look that passed between them.

Maximus scrambled over the back of the mountain wagon. He crawled over the supplies to the rear of the wagon, puffing with exertion, and onto the canvas bags stamped "salt."

"Here you are," he said, pulling at the bag lying on top.

"How do I know there's salt in it?" Fargo asked.

A flash of relief crossed Sweedler's face and he said, "Oh, there's salt alright."

"I'd like to see that," Fargo said.

With a look of triumph, Sweedler fished a pocketknife out of the tight pocket of his green-striped pants and opened the blade. He expertly slit open the white stitching on the top of the bag and pulled the sides apart.

Fargo moved the pinto closer to the wagon and stood up in the stirrups to look down into the bag. Inside was the gray mottled salt.

"Fine," Fargo said. "But, I don't want a bag that's been opened."

Maximus started.

"Fine, fine," he said and bent to pull up the second bag.

"No, I want one from down on the bottom," Fargo said, pointing. "Way down at the bottom."

"Take this one," Sweedler whined. "They're all the same."

"The bottom ones might have more . . . minerals," Fargo said.

"Give him what he wants," hissed Wilhelmina impatiently. "Then we can be on our way."

Maximus panted with the effort of moving the forty-pound sacks aside, offering several of them to Fargo. Skye noticed that the bags on top were stitched with white thread, but the ones from the bottom were closed with black thread.

"No," Fargo said. "I want one of those at the bottom."

Finally, Maximus got one with black thread. He lifted it toward the edge of the wagon.

"How do I know this one has salt in it?" Fargo asked.

"Open it for him," said Wilhelmina.

Maximus hesitated and then slowly slit open the bag. Fargo looked inside. As he suspected, the salt was dirtier than the other bag he had looked into. They had mixed the gold dust with the salt. With both of them working at it, the job would have taken only an hour. And Wilhelmina's deft fingers would have quickly sewn the bags shut.

He straightened up immediately, after only a glance.

"Looks just fine," he said. "Except, I'd like an unopened bag."

Maximus breathed a sigh, which sounded like relief, and turned back to grasp one of the bags on the top of the heap.

"No," Fargo said. "That one." He pointed to one with black thread.

Maximus reluctantly brought it to the edge of the wagon.

Fargo thought as he watched the fat salesman struggle with the bag. What other way was there to get under the skin of Maximus Sweedler? What could he do to Maximus's ointments that would irritate the hell out of him? Of course . . . Fargo grinned.

"While I'm shopping, I'd like a few of your medicines too," Fargo said. "Say ten or fifteen ought to do us."

"Ten or fifteen!" Maximus echoed, suddenly excited. "But what are your symptoms? What kind of curatives might I provide? Whatever ails you, my friend? What . . ."

"Never mind," said Fargo. He rode the pinto toward the cart and removed his hat, plucking fifteen of the smallest bottles from the leather loops and placing them inside his hat. He handed the hat to Maximus.

"What the hell?" Sam exclaimed.

"Add that to my bill," he said. "How much more do I owe you?"

"Eight dollars and forty-two cents," Maximus answered. "Plus fifty dollars for the salt."

Fargo paid him and handed the hat to Sam.

"Now for my salt," he said. Fargo moved the pinto flush against the wagon and Maximus tipped the large bag over the edge. Fargo eased the bag down and arranged it across the saddle in front of him.

"And now you'lll get us out of here?" said Maximus.

"Sure," Fargo said. "In a little while. C'mon, Sam."

They rode toward the bank, Sam in the lead. Just as they approached the bank, Fargo gave the bag of salt a shove. It fell off the saddle and into the shallows. The canvas bag rested on the bottom of the moving stream, covered by running water.

"Oh, look what I've done!" Fargo said in mock horror. "I wonder how much salt will be left in that bag after the water runs through it for a while? Say about half an hour . . ."

Sam chuckled as he got off the bay.

Fargo turned back to look at the Sweedlers. Wilhelmina's eyes blazed with fury as she sat atop the wagon, surrounded by the rushing water. Maximus was making his shaky way back to the driver's seat.

Fargo dismounted on the bank.

"What did you buy this trash for?" asked Sam, holding Fargo's hat in his hands. He looked down at the jumble of small patent-medicine bottles.

"I thought we'd need something to do while the salt washes away from that gold dust," Fargo said.

Sam looked at him quizzically.

"What? Sit around and drink that dadburned stuff?"

"Target practice," said Skye. Sam guffawed until he began to wheeze and Fargo slapped him on the back.

"Old Maximus is going to love sitting in the middle of that river and watching this," said Sam, catching his breath. "I'll set 'em up. But fifteen bottles aren't going to last long."

"Set 'em up real far away," said Fargo. "Say, in a row over on that log yonder. First we'll shoot the corks out. Then we'll carve off the stems. Then plug the bottles."

"Yeah," said Sam, walking toward the stump. "That could kill some time pleasantly."

The last of the bottles standing on the log exploded in a glittering shower of liquid medicine and glass. Sam whooped.

"Good shootin'," Sam said. "This target practice has given me a new respect for snake oil."

"How about a little gold panning?" Fargo said with a smile. He glanced over at the Sweedlers, as he had many times during the last hour, to see them still sitting infuriated on their wagon, in the middle of the creek.

Fargo waded in and pulled the canvas bag toward the shore. It was noticeably emptier than it had been, the canvas looser around the weight within. He dragged it onto the grassy bank, pulled the throwing knife from his ankle holster and slit open the black threads on the top of the bag.

Sam eagerly plunged his hand in. His hand emerged glittering with dark golden flakes. He opened it and on the palm was a small heap of glistening, gold dust, dark and wet.

"What do you think that is, Sam?" Fargo asked in a loud voice.

"There's gold in them there bag," Sam replied, scraping the wet dust off his hands back into the bag.

"Interesting!" Fargo said, keeping his voice loud enough to carry over the rushing water.

"Th—there's what?" Maximus shouted.

"Shut up, you fool," Wilhelmina said quietly to her husband.

Fargo straightened up.

"Come on, Sam."

Now that they were absolutely sure, it was time to secure these two and get back to Denver City. He strode to the Ovaro and mounted, guiding the horse into the stream toward the Sweedler's wagon. Sam followed.

As he neared the wagon, Maximus suddenly stood, his eyes large with fear and his round body quaking. He turned and scrambled over the goods in the wagon, then jumped off the rear. Fargo followed, riding alongside the wagon. Above the roar of the water, he suddenly heard a distinctive click and he hunched down, drew and twisted about in one fast motion.

The shot whizzed close by his left ear, in a hot explosion of sound and he watched, as if in slow motion, the pistol fly out of Wilhelmina's hands, his bullet having caught the barrel as it lifted from the kickback.

She cried out in pain, grasping her wrenched hand, her eyes as dark as a storm, flashing with furious lightning.

"Wilhelmina!" Fargo heard Maximus call out. He saw the man splashing back toward the driver's seat and climbing aboard to sit beside his wife. "Are you shot?" he asked her, breathlessly.

She shook her head, speechless with frustration and fury.

Maximus put his arm around his wife.

"I told you it wouldn't work," he said in a low voice. "We did just fine selling ointments."

Fargo rode toward the wagon, loosening his rope. He jumped aboard.

"Let me see your hand," he said to Mrs. Sweedler.

"Leave me alone," she said, as vicious as a cornered wild animal. Fargo gently laid his hand on her arm and pulled the hand toward him, examining it closely. There was no break in the skin. His bullet had struck her pistol and the impact had sprained her wrist. He saw a purplish swelling beginning.

"Move your fingers," he said. She did. "Fetch a couple of splints, Sam." Fargo quickly splinted her wrist with his bandana while she watched him with a puzzled look.

"Sorry I have to do this," Fargo said, when he had finished. He pulled the rope from his saddle and bound the Sweedlers together, being careful to keep the ropes loose for circulation.

Sam had fished Wilhelmina's pistol out of the stream. He began to lead the mules back into the water, to hitch them to the wagon. When the team was assembled, with Bessietoo in the lead, Sam hitched his bay to the back of the painted cart and waded around to climb up on the wagon's driver seat, alongside the Sweedlers.

Fargo sat on his horse on the bank watching as Sam flapped the reins and said some low words to the mule team, which moved forward slowly and steadily, pulling the heavy wagons up the bank. At the top of the rise, on a broad grassy area, Sam turned the team and the wagons in a wide circle and headed south, back through the water of the Big Thompson River and toward Denver City.

Fargo pushed through the batwing doors of Fanny's. It was crowded. Soldiers clustered by the bar. Three card games were in progress and Fanny's girls were scurrying everywhere with drinks and trays of food. Fanny pushed out of the kitchen door and sighted Fargo across the room. Her face brightened and she bustled over.

"Paul will be glad to see you back. Any luck?"

"Sure. Got 'em outside."

Fanny pushed open one of the swinging doors and peered out.

"What a pretty sight!" she said. "Trussed up like two turkeys, fit to be broiled. Never did like those two swindlers."

"Sweedlers," Fargo said. "Know where the sheriff is?"

"He was in here for supper," Fanny said, looking around the room, "but I think he's gone back to the jail house."

Fanny started as she looked out at the street. "There's Paul now."

They hurried out and met Cavendish walking toward the Sweedler's wagons.

"Fargo! Good hunting I see."

Maximus and Wilhelmina sat on the wagon beside Sam, silent and beyond protesting.

"The dust is mixed in with the salt. It's all in the back of the wagon," Fargo said. "But I think we should get these two locked up for the night."

"I'd best get back to my customers," Fanny said. "Nice seeing you again." She nodded toward the Sweedlers.

Fargo and Cavendish walked toward the jail house, followed by Sam driving the wagon.

"Any news about the decoy team? Have they been ambushed yet?" Fargo asked, keeping his voice low.

"No word from Wyatt yet," Cavendish answered. "Why don't you go get some supper and a rest? Sam and I can take care of this."

Fargo didn't protest and moved off toward Fanny's. Then he remembered something and turned back.

"You might want to send for the doc to take a look at Mrs. Sweedler's wrist," he said.

"Your dinner is upstairs in your room," Fanny said. "And I've ordered a hot bath. The girls will bring up the jugs in a half hour."

"Sounds great," Fargo said. He began to climb the stairs.

"Skye," Fanny called. He turned back and she took several steps up to stand close beside him. "I just want to let you know something. That girl . . . the one with the brown hair . . ." she said in a low voice, disapproval written in the furrows on her brow.

"Prudence?" he asked.

"Well, I don't know . . . of course, it's none of my business . . ." she muttered and then broke off.

"What is it, Fanny?" he asked.

"Well, that hussy in the eyeglasses has been in here by herself all day."

"So?"

"She's not with that Booth fellow, I mean to say," Fanny said meaningfully. "The sheriff told him to leave town."

"So?"

"So, she's been asking everybody where you are. Now,

120

why would she be looking for you? Maybe because she had to break off with Booth?'' Fanny said. She threw up her hands. "Don't answer me, Skye. If you're planning to two-time Laurel, I don't want to know."

"Did Prudence find out where I'd gone?" Fargo asked in a serious tone, ignoring Fanny's remarks.

"I doubt it," Fanny said, catching his tone. "Those that knew—me, Paul, and Laurel—weren't talking."

"So she's been asking about me. Interesting," Fargo said thoughtfully. "Thanks for telling me. I'll keep it in mind." He started up the stairs. "Oh, Fanny," he added, turning. "If you run into Prudence again, just tell her my dance card's full for the moment."

Fanny nodded and winked.

"I'd be happy to give her that message," she said.

He climbed the stairway toward his room. As he turned the white china knob on the door, he heard a rustle inside. He drew his Colt revolver and pushed open the door.

8

Laurel's face turned pale as she saw the barrel of his revolver. He holstered it quickly.

"Wasn't expecting you," he said, crossing the room and folding her into his arms.

"I thought you'd need some help washing your back."

"Absolutely," he agreed, seeing the copper tub waiting to be filled. A table was set with two suppers. "But let's eat."

Laurel laughed when he told her about Maximus and Wilhelmina stranded on their wagon in the middle of the Big Thompson River.

"I wish I could have seen their faces!" she said. "Serves them right."

"Actually," Skye said, "they're not such bad sorts. They were just two small people who suddenly got greedy. The really dangerous ones burn with greed. They want gold at any price. They'll sell their souls for it. You meet a lot of those types out here. They can be very deceptive."

Laurel shivered. "Let's get you cleaned up," she said.

He arose from the steaming water now black with the soot from the night before and the dust of the trail. Laurel handed him a rough cotton towel.

"I certainly did get wet scrubbing you down," she said, with a hint of shyness. "I'd better slip out of these soaked clothes."

Tired as he was, Fargo could feel the stirring in him and she noticed. He dried his lean and muscular body as she unbuttoned her skirt and slipped out of her blouse. Laurel wore lacy bloomers and a thin camisole, through which he could see the round outline of her breasts.

As Skye and Laurel tumbled onto the bed, she wrapped her arms about him, then sprang back.

"Didn't you dry off your back?" she admonished, rising and fetching the towel.

"Guess I'm just the helpless type," he said, as he rolled lazily onto his side and let her finish drying him. After a moment, he didn't feel the towel anymore, but felt her stretched out beside him on the bed, her hand softly rubbing his tired muscles, then massaging him as he relaxed, then exploring and finding. He turned toward her, ready, nibbled her shoulders, her nipples, her warm mouth, inhaling her fresh citrus scent. He pulled her bloomers down gently as she opened to him.

He felt the pulsing desire in him and held back, as he slowly entered her warmth, brushing her lips with his. Her gray eyes were wide open and smiling into his.

"Yes, Skye, yes," she said and he felt the restraint lifted as he thrust again and again. She lifted her small lithe body against his, until the pulsing world swam in front of his eyes and he felt it slipping, crashing. He pushed again, shuddering and felt her trembling beneath him in ecstasy, riding it out together with him and around him. He sank forward onto her, feeling her mouth's small kisses on him as he sank into sleep.

"Laurel . . ." he heard himself say.

The morning breeze fluttered the curtains when he awoke. Laurel lay in the crook of his arm, her blond hair strewn over the pillow and glittering in a patch of sunlight. Fargo rose and dressed quietly. It was hot inside the room and he went to the window, opening the sash further to catch the breeze.

The sound of approaching hoofbeats drummed through the still morning and he heard shouting. He leaned out the window and looked down the street. What the hell was going on?

A group of men, about twenty of them, rode toward Fanny's. The band was bristling with rifles and pistols and ammunition. As they drew closer, Fargo recognized the brown-bearded man named Budge Hays and two other men who had guarded the barricade the day before. They came to a halt in front of Fanny's.

"Come on!" Budge shouted. "Let's go get us some Indian flesh."

"Hey you!" Fargo shouted down to the man, who turned around in the street on his horse several times, trying to locate the voice. "Up here!" The man looked up, squinting in the sun.

"Where do you think you're going?" Fargo asked.

"What's it to ya?" Budge Hays replied. Several more men appeared below, untied their horses and mounted, joining the group.

"It's nothing to me," Fargo said nonchalantly. "But if you're looking for Indians, I'd better warn you that there are a couple hundred of them."

Fargo saw the group shift nervously at his words. Even from the distance of the second story, Fargo could see the red flush of fury—or was it Taos Lightning?—in the bearded man's cheeks.

"I'm no yeller belly!" the man growled. "We've got good rifles. I say one of us can kill a dozen of those animals. We ain't forgetting Gates and his wife. We ain't forgetting what those Indians did. We're gonna teach them a lesson they won't forget!"

There were rumbles of approval from the group of men.

"I told you, they weren't Arapaho," Fargo protested. "They were Crow."

"There ain't no difference," Hays said. "I ain't scared of Indians. One thing I'd like to know. Where was Mister Skye Fargo the night when we were under siege?"

"I rode out to spy on them. And I tell you, the Arapaho are peaceful."

"That's what you say," Budge spit back. "I say you ran and hid. Left the rest of us to defend the town. Come on, boys. Let's go teach those Indians a lesson. Let's go!"

Budge lay the quirt heavily across the neck of his big white, which reared and then galloped down the street.

The rest of the men followed, some looking up toward Fargo as they rode by under his window. Clearly, many of them were reluctant to go along but afraid of being called a coward if they did not.

Fargo leaned out the window to look after them until he could see and hear them no longer. The dust settled and the street was quiet. He swore under his breath at the stupidity of fear as he wondered how many of the men, if any, would return to Denver City.

The gold shipment had to be moved and the sooner the better. There had been a day's delay already in going after the Sweedlers.

There was even greater need for haste now. If Budge Hays and these vigilantes stirred up the Indians, it would only cause more trouble on the trail for Fargo and Sam. He must leave immediately, he realized.

He turned from the window and saw that Laurel had awakened and was propped up on the bed, watching him.

"Did you hear that?" he asked.

"The whole thing," she said, shaking her head. "I heard Father say that Budge Hays is always stirring up trouble. What does it all mean?"

"It might mean a lot of things. One thing it means for sure. Sam and I have to get a move on. Now," Fargo said.

"And afterward?" she asked.

Fargo grinned. "I'll be back for my . . . reward." He bent over and kissed her good-bye.

Behind the Auraria Private Mint was an enclosed loading yard, accessible by double wooden gates on the main street and on a back alley. The mint's loading yard was usually bustling during the day, but this afternoon, it stood deserted except for the mountain wagon loaded with prospecting gear.

Paul Cavendish, Sam, and Fargo stood on one side of the wagon.

"I packed the boxes with the gold ingots myself," Cavendish said. "Sam and I had no trouble loading them into the bottom of the wagon."

"I wouldn't call it no trouble," Sam said ruefully, rubbing his lower back.

"The gold's in five locked chests, hidden under all your other gear," Cavendish said. "I'll let you out the back gate. I doubt anyone will see you. I'll make sure that rumor circulates town in a day or two that you went off prospecting."

"Good," Fargo said.

"Once you're on the trail, just keep a lookout for those bandits. Whoever they are," Cavendish said.

"And Indians on the rampage," Fargo said.

"What?" Paul said.

Fargo filled him in on the vigilante group that had just ridden out of Denver City.

"I heard those horses go by when we were loading," Sam said. "We were in too much of a hurry to go have a look."

"All the more reason for haste," Fargo said. "With hard driving and some backtracking to hide our tracks, we can be out of Arapaho territory in two days."

"Let's git," said Sam, climbing aboard. Fargo mounted his pinto.

Paul opened the tall clapboard gates at the back of the yard and Sam clucked to the mule team, which stood stock still. Fargo noticed that a familiar mule with very long ears led the team.

"Sam, don't I know that mule from somewhere?"

Sam grinned. "Bought her off the sheriff," he said. "Perfectly legal like."

He flapped the reins again, confidently, but the team took no notice.

"Dammit, honey, don't give me trouble! Skedaddle!" he said, flapping the reins across their backs.

One of the mules turned its head and gave Sam a baleful look.

Sam clambered down, swearing under his breath, and went to the front of the line while Fargo and Cavendish waited. Sam bent over and whispered something into Bessietoo's long ear which twitched several times. Then Sam climbed aboard and flapped the reins. The team moved forward.

"What in hell did you say to that mule?" Fargo asked Sam, as he followed the heavy wagon out of the wide gate into the alleyway.

"Told her I knew a snake-oil salesman who might want a mule if she didn't move her ass."

Fargo heard Cavendish chuckling as he shut the gate behind them.

"Good luck!" Paul called out to them quietly.

The streets of Denver City were almost deserted; many of the towns people were down by Cherry Creek cleaning up from the flood. They rode through the center of town, Fargo following the wagon, toward the head of the trail southward to Pike's Peak. The buildings became fewer and fewer and then the trail lay before them, curving and thinning to nothingness toward the horizon.

As the wagon crawled out onto the plains, Sam fumbled in his kit and brought out the silver-worked cow horn. He put it to his lips. It sputtered and then gave a low, mournful call.

Out of the corner of his eyes, the Trailsman sighted the lone horseman trailing them as soon as they climbed the first rise out of Denver City. Fargo did not look back, but rode on ahead of the wagon, turning back from time to time to talk to Sam and note the horseman behind them.

Fargo was surprised to see how recklessly the rider approached the crests of the hills behind them and rode into full view several times. From what Fargo could tell, the rider only occasionally took advantage of the available cover provided by the stands of rabbit bush and clumps of thick sage.

Either the man wanted to be seen, or he was a damned poor tracker, Fargo decided. He reined in until he trotted beside the wagon. "We're being followed, but don't turn around. Behind us is some tenderfoot tracker."

"You gonna ride back and see who it is?" Sam asked.

"No. Let's press on. When we're camped for the night, I'll pay a surprise visit."

At nightfall, they stopped in a tiny clearing among low sage in the bottom of an arroyo. Sam unloaded the bedrolls and his frying pan while Fargo wandered a short distance away to gather dry twigs and bark. He heard a horse snort from behind them and knew the tracker was very close. No need to hurry, he thought. It was another moonless night. Fargo laid a small fire, hot and smokeless, while Sam sliced bacon and stirred something in a pan. They had spoken very little, tired from the trail.

"Guess I'll lie down for a while," Fargo said in a loud, clear voice, with a glance at Sam. Sam nodded. Fargo pulled the bedroll away from the fire into the deeper shadows and lay down on it. After a moment, he rolled off it, bunched up the bedroll so it didn't lay flat, and then slipped into the sage.

He moved quietly, hand on his revolver, ears alert and eyes quickly adjusting to the night. He made a wide circle around the point from where he had heard the horse snort, and then approached from behind. He came upon a sorrel, picketed to a low bush. It was straining to reach a patch of grass which lay just out of reach. It nickered as it smelled him approach and he melted backward into the sage, giving the horse a wide berth.

Now he was moving on a course between the horse and the campsite, ears straining to catch any sound. He heard the crunching of gravel—someone walking before him toward the fire. He crept up behind the sound until he saw a short dark figure ahead of him. He followed, soundlessly, as the figure approached the campsite. Ahead, he heard Sam whistling tunelessly through his teeth. There was the pop of bacon and then the smell of it. The dark figure paused and drew up behind a bush, parting the branches with both hands to peer through.

Fargo jumped. He pinned the tracker's arms immediately, throwing him off his feet and onto the ground. The tracker was slender and weak, but fought like a fury, clawing at his face. Fargo wrapped his arms about the small body and felt, with a shock, the unmistakable softness of a woman. He pulled her to her feet and pushed her forward into the fire-light, dashing the hat off her head.

Brown curls tumbled out. Wide, frightened brown eyes, like a deer's, met his.

"Prudence!" he said.

"Oh, brother," said Sam. "Female trouble."

"Why in hell are you following us?" Fargo asked her.

She bent down to retrieve her hat and then stood, twisting it in her hands.

"There's just nothing for me in Denver City, Skye. I . . . I heard you were going away. Gold . . . gold prospecting,

I heard. And I thought I would follow you and . . . and ask you to take me with you.''

"What's Matthew Booth going to think about you running off like this?" Fargo asked.

"Why do you ask about Ma . . . Mister Booth?" she asked.

"Well, you and he seemed sweet on each other, from what I could see in Denver City," Fargo said. She was nervous as a rabbit in a snare. "Or is that all over now?"

"He has nothing to do with this!" she protested, anger in her eyes.

Fargo watched her, considering. He couldn't send her back to Denver City alone. If the vigilantes had attacked the Arapaho, the tribe would go on a killing spree and find her alone on the plains. Neither he nor Sam could accompany her back to Denver City either. They would lose valuable time. The only thing to do was to keep going forward. And take her along.

But Fargo didn't like it. And he could tell, by Sam's look—one eye screwed up and peering at the girl—that he liked it even less. But there was nothing else to be done.

"You come with us," Fargo said. "For the moment."

"I won't be any trouble," she said.

"Women are bad luck on a prospecting expedition," Sam muttered. He shot a sideways look at Fargo, who nodded. They had just agreed to keep the real reason for their journey a secret from Pru.

"I'll get your horse," Fargo said, and retraced his steps. The sorrel had broken free and was happily grazing in the grassy patch.

"There's better stuff down by us," Fargo said absent-mindedly to the horse as he led him toward the campsite. Of course, he thought, it would be impossible to keep Pru from guessing that something was afoot. The next morning they would come upon the turnoff to Pike's Peak. There, Fargo planned to lay a false trail and then backtrack, heading east. How would he explain that? Well, he would think of something. But he couldn't imagine what.

Sam was quietly sulking, after they finished the meal. He

129

cleared up and then looked meaningfully toward the bedrolls, raising his eyebrows toward Fargo with a wry smile.

"Take my bedroll," Fargo said to Pru.

She was too tired to protest. She stood up slowly and made her way toward it. Fargo took an extra blanket and rolled himself inside it beside the fire. His last image was of Sam, getting ready to lie down, shaking his head and muttering.

Before dawn, they were on the trail again, Pru riding on the wagon beside Sam, the sorrel hitched behind, and Fargo on the pinto. The morning was clear and cool—a cloudless blue sky was overhead and Pike's Peak rising cool white before them.

As he rode, Fargo heard Pru's voice talking to Sam. Then he heard Sam's guffaw. It was impossible not to be charmed by her. But Fargo felt uneasy. The danger was almost upon them. He knew it. He could feel it creeping up on them. Or it lay in wait ahead of them. All he could do was hurry. Hurry.

By midmorning, they had reached the junction with the Pike's Peak trail. Fargo signalled Sam to steer the wagon toward one side and saw with satisfaction the deep wheel tracks left in the soft earth beside the hard-packed trail, showing clearly which way they had gone. Just in case someone was following.

Fargo led them up the Pike's Peak trail, which plunged into a deep canyon dark-green with pine. Ahead were the hidden culverts and clear streams leading up into the high country, and the obscure valleys which had enticed hundreds of gold prospectors. It had been a while since Fargo had been up this trail, but he remembered it well.

They reached the crossing where the trail dipped into a shallow stream, babbling with snowmelt, and then climbed, becoming suddenly rocky. Fargo remembered the track ahead, steep and rocky for more than a mile before leveling off again.

He rode the Ovaro into the streambed and dismounted, feeling the cold water fill his boots. As the mule team entered the stream, Fargo guided them gently toward downstream, turning the team.

"Where are we going?" he heard Pru shout.

Fargo looked up to see Sam shrug his shoulders at her.

The water was broad and shallow, barely reaching the spokes of the wagon, the streambed pebbly and flat. He gestured to Sam who handed the reins to Pru and jumped into the stream, helping to guide the mules along the streambed. It was tough going, the mules fumbling for footing, the wagon bumping over the rounded stones.

Fargo strode to the bank over which they had driven into the stream. In the glittering gravel beside the creek, four wheel tracks, overlapping to form two wide tracks, led straight into the water. He noted the depth and the width. He waded to the other side of the creek and dug out matching tracks a few feet up the bank until he reached the rocky trail. He scrambled some rocks there. Then he filled his hat with water and splashed it up the bank, again and again, and stood back to survey his work.

It was a lot of trouble to go to just in case they were being followed. The conspirators might have taken the bait and followed Roundtree, Fargo thought. Or maybe they didn't. If somebody was tracking them, they would probably ride up the steep rocky trail ahead for several miles before they would discover that there were no fresh tracks. Then they would have to double back, examining the trail all the way.

But if they suspected anything when they crossed the stream and dismounted for a close examination, they would see that the tracks had been dug out, not made by the weight of a mountain wagon. And no fresh mule tracks. All the trick could do was gain them some time.

He must not linger on the trail, in case someone rode by. The mountain wagon was already out of sight around the bend, driving downstream. Fargo followed.

A quarter mile downstream, the water passed over a shelf of solid rock, which flowed like hardened liquid down from the side of the mountain. The mules hauled the wagon out of the stream and onto the flat naked rock. Fargo rode up beside the wagon.

"Will you tell me what's going on?" Pru asked. Fargo heard a note of fear in her voice.

"We want to make sure we aren't being followed," Fargo said.

"Oh," Pru said. She opened her mouth to say more, but then thought better of it.

"A lot of people want to know where Sweeteye Sam is going to make his next big strike," Sam said. "We're taking a detour to throw 'em off our trail."

Pru nodded thoughtfully. Fargo knew that explanation wouldn't satisfy her for long. Especially when they headed due east, away from Pike's Peak. He led the wagon across the rock-flow shelf and onto an old grassy Indian track, just wide enough for the wagon, which would take them back to the plains. They emerged from the pine trees at the foot of the hills in midafternoon.

"Do you think we can stop for something to eat?" Pru asked. Fargo had noticed that she was continually looking behind them. Was it nervousness or something else? He didn't like it.

"Not for a while," he said. "We need to put a few miles behind us."

They drove hard for an hour more, the mules making steady time across the wide track in the buffalo grass, heading east under the broad sky until the mountains grew slightly smaller behind them. Pru had said nothing on the drive east, but her face became more and more grim.

It was late afternoon when they halted by a brook for a quick repast, pulling the wagon into a gentle depression on the plains so it could not be seen from far away. Sam fetched water while Fargo laid a quick fire. It was just burning, hot and smokeless, when Sam returned.

"There's a trout pool upstream," Sam said excitedly.

"No time, Sam."

"I'll be just a moment. We can eat 'em tonight."

"Alright, but be quick. We get back on the trail in half an hour. I'll take care of the animals," Fargo said.

"I'll . . . watch the fire," Pru said.

He led the mules a short distance away, over a small rise and down by the brook where there was a wide bank and tender grass. He had just picketed the last mule when he heard Pru come up behind him. She sidled around to stand in front of him and put one hand out to pet the mule.

"How come you're ignoring me, Skye?" she asked, her round brown eyes troubled.

"We're in a hurry," he said. "I'm not ignoring you."

"You are," she said, pouting.

Skye examined her face. What was she after? This was no time for games. He shrugged and started to turn back. He felt her hand, suddenly strong and insistent on his arm.

'What is it, Pru?''

"Skye, sometimes people do things that they don't want to. They do something they regret, but maybe it's for love."

"What are you getting at, Pru?" he asked.

"Would you kiss me, Skye? Just once?"

"Look, Pru . . ."

"Well, you seemed to like it before. What happened?"

Fargo thought of how she had been that night at the Seventeen Mile House—warm, funny, and wanting. Then he thought of the complications, of her taking Matthew Booth's hand in the saloon and patting his cheek. She was certainly forward. And fun. But she didn't seem to have much common sense. What was she doing with a man like Booth?

Pru wasn't like Laurel, he thought. He understood Laurel thoroughly. There was something about Prudence that was unpredictable, like a wild card that might turn up in the middle of a game. Yet, for all that, he still liked her.

She was looking up at him expectantly, her soft mouth still pouting, her wide brown eyes watching him. He bent over to kiss her and heard the deep call of Sam's horn.

Fargo wheeled about. A thick column of smoke billowed upward, gray and black swirling into the clear blue sky—a thousand-foot-high sign which said, "Here we are."

"You were supposed to watch the fire!" he heard himself snap at Pru, as he ran toward it, angry at her, angry at himself for being distracted.

He arrived at the same time as Sam. They looked down and saw the thick layer of wet green grass which had been thrown on top of the burning dry twigs.

9

Sam threw himself down on the ground and began to pluck the wet grass out of the flames, swearing as he burned his fingers.

"Bitch," Fargo said. Pru couldn't be that stupid. On the contrary, she was that clever. The wet grass on the fire wasn't an accident.

"Goddamn women," Sam said, as he continued to pull the wet grass from the fire. "Bad luck. Stick to mules."

"Won't do much good now, Sam," Fargo said, his voice low and his mouth a thin line. "Get your rifles loaded and get in the wagon. I'll go find out what the hell is going on."

Fargo turned and ran toward the creek and the mules, where he had left Pru. She was nowhere in sight. The hoofprints of her sorrel led upstream. He jumped onto the Ovaro and followed through the rabbit bush. He came upon her in a clearing, standing beside her mount, her head resting on one of the flanks. Obviously, she had meant to run but something held her back. He dismounted, seized her arm and jerked her around to face him. Tears stained her cheeks. Her eyes grew frightened as she saw the menace in his eyes.

"What the hell are you doing? Who's the signal for?"

Pru winced at his painful grasp on her arm, but she tightened her lips and looked at him wordlessly. He'd have to scare it out of her, he thought. He wished what he was about to say was only a ploy to get her to talk. Unfortunately, he realized, it might very well happen.

"Suit yourself," Fargo said. "But we may not have much time before the Indians get here."

She started. "Indians?"

"Oh, maybe you hadn't heard. Budge Hays and a bunch

of the Denver City boys formed a vigilante gang and took off yesterday. Mad about what happened to Gates and his wife. By now they've probably killed a bunch of innocent Arapaho. The Arapaho didn't kill Gates. But they won't sit still when they've been attacked. They're going to be looking around for some scalps. Any scalps.''

"Oh my god!'' Pru said, looking about her wildly. "Oh my god! What will we do? Shouldn't we run for it?''

"Won't do us any good. That smoke can be seen for miles. Anyone looking for us is already heading this way. Our only chance is to dig in.''

There was a chance, he thought, that Budge Hays hadn't found the Arapaho camp yet. In that case, the Indians would leave them in peace. He knew it was a small chance. But who else was looking for them and waiting for Pru's smoke signal?

"Why the smoke?''

"Skye . . . I . . . I . . .'' She shook her head and buried her face in her hands, sobbing. He grasped her arms and shook her.

"Come on, Pru. There's not much time.''

"I . . . I . . . can't. He's innocent, I swear.''

Fargo thought about the sullen dark man with the angry eyes.

"Booth.''

She looked up and nodded. Just then Fargo heard Sam's low horn speak again.

Fargo jumped onto the pinto and pulled Pru up behind him, put his spur to the horse and galloped over the rise back to the wagon. In the distance, he saw a group of riders, like a dark swarm of insects on the far horizon. They weren't Indians.

Fargo slid down and pulled Pru off the pony. He slapped the horse on the rump and it cantered over the hill. It wouldn't wander far, he knew. The mules were tethered by the brook, safely out of firing range. They would have to fight it out. No running. Sam was tossing gear out of the center of the loaded wagon, clearing a space for them to stand, piling the remaining gear on all sides for cover.

"Get inside,'' Fargo directed Pru.

He jumped up into the wagon after her and helped Sam pile more of the heavy gear about them. They feverishly lifted two of the heavy wooden boxes from the mint one on top of another.

"Great protection from bullets," Sam said, winking at Fargo as they lifted up the last box of ingots. They could hear the pounding hoofs clearly. Fargo took one last look around. The wooden boxes of gold ingots were piled in two places, with the bags and piles of assorted gear between giving them some protection. By raising their heads, they had a full-circle view all about them.

"Get between us, Pru," Fargo said, changing places with her. "Here in the middle. No matter what happens, keep your head down." He felt her tremble as he pressed by her. Now he was in the forward end of the wagon, Sam in back.

"We have the advantage," Fargo said to Sam. "They'll be shooting from moving horses. With luck, we can pick off a good number of them in the first charge."

At his words, the band came into full view over the hill. Fargo counted fourteen—professionals by the look of them, with their trail-broken saddles and their range rifles. A familiar figure drew Fargo's attention at once, a tall man in the back of the group. He swore under his breath. Innocent? he thought. Matthew Booth riding with bandits was hardly innocent.

"Fire," Fargo said quietly and he and Sam opened up. Fargo shot with both rifles, one in each hand. Three of the bandits fell at once. One, just winged, crawled into a nearby bush. Fargo made a note to keep an eye on him as they reloaded and the first fusillade hit the wagon. He heard the dull click of one bullet striking metal. One of Cavendish's ingots, he thought. He heard Sam chuckle.

"That barrier's worth its weight in gold," Sam said while loading.

Fargo's next round caught two more, dead center. One of the men fell, his foot caught in a stirrup, and was dragged through the brush by his mount. He heard more bullets hitting the metal ingots in the boxes. Sam fired off another round and caught one man in a brown leather hat, who slumped forward in his saddle, the horse pulling up short and standing confused among the gunfire.

Fargo saw a movement in the brush where the wounded man had crawled. A rifle barrel protruded, aimed at Sam. Fargo fired both rifles into the foliage. The barrel sank slowly, then fired into the dirt, kicking up a fan of dust.

The bandits had lost six men in short order, almost half their number. Booth raised his hand and they retreated out of range. Fargo watched as they pulled into a tight circle, glancing over their shoulders from time to time toward the wagon.

"They'll circle us Indian style. Or they'll think up some kind of cover," Fargo guessed. He reloaded his rifles and checked the catch on his pistol as he spoke, watching the dark group carefully. A cry went up from them as they broke, riding out one by one.

"Indian style it is," Fargo said, aiming at a tall fellow in a checkered shirt and bringing him down. Two more fell, one his and one Sam's, in quick succession. But now the shots were zinging all around them. It was only a matter of time. The encirclement made it harder to keep cover. Fargo ducked as a shot whizzed by from behind and he felt his hair singed by its passing.

Another of the bandits fell as Sam said, "Got him. Four left, plus Booth. You get Booth, and I'll get that big fella on the bay."

"Right," Fargo muttered, aligning his rifle with the moving figure of Matthew Booth.

Before he could pull the trigger, a pig-eyed man galloped close and took slow aim at Sam. A shot zinged and Sam cried out. Fargo glanced over to see him clutching his chest.

"Jesus," Sam said. The blood began to seep through his fingers.

"Sam!" Pru said, moving toward him. Skye glimpsed her loosening Sam's grip on his rifle as he turned away. He scanned for the dark tall form of Booth.

An instant later, the blow fell, the surprise as painful as the pain itself, a sharp crack on the back of his skull which made the afternoon sky tilt and whirl, filled with blazing, winking suns. As Skye staggered and fell, he turned to see, with bleary eyes, Pru standing above him, holding Sam's rifle by its barrel.

* * *

The ground came slowly into focus. His legs were stretched out in front of him, bound, his hands tied painfully tight behind his back. He turned his wrists. No give. A professional job. His Colt revolver was gone. He rubbed his legs together. His throwing knife was gone, unstrapped from his ankle. A real professional job.

On one side of him he felt the rough texture of a pile of canvas and the hardness of a wooden cask—part of the pile of gear he and Sam had jettisoned in the moments before the bandits rode up. On the other side, he felt the warmth of a body beside him and he moved his head very slowly.

Sam lay on the ground next to him, bound and unconscious, a dark stain down the front of his shirt. Fargo listened and was relieved to hear the old prospector's steady and deep breathing. The bullet had not punctured a lung. Nor had it hit Sam's heart. With any luck it had passed clean through the shoulder, in which case he would recover. Fargo moved his head slowly back to center and kept still, his eyes half closed, listening.

Booth and Pru stood in front of him, not far away. The other men were not in sight, but he heard their voices from the direction of the creek and he guessed they were watering their horses and rounding up the mule team. The dead men lay where they had fallen. The bandits had not moved the bodies.

"I didn't know you were in the wagon," Booth was saying. "You were supposed to give the signal and then ride away."

"Well, it's over now," Pru said, her voice indistinct and tremulous. "I was worried you'd lose the trail up near Pike's Peak."

"We were almost to the junction leading into the canyon when we saw the smoke out east," Booth said. "Another ten minutes and we'd have been in the mountains and missed it."

"Now we can rescue the gold and clear your name! Everything will be fine."

Fargo opened his eyes fully.

"I wouldn't say this theft will clear the name of Matthew Booth," Fargo said.

Booth whirled about.

"Theft?" Pru asked. "Skye, you don't understand. Matthew is not the criminal. Paul Cavendish is."

Fargo shifted himself against the wagon wheel and looked up at her narrowly.

"Would you like to explain that to me? Slowly. Real slowly."

"It's a set up," Pru said. "Matthew told me all about it. You see, Matthew found out that Cavendish was really sending the gold with you. Wyatt Roundtree and his team were just to mislead everybody."

"Big news," Fargo said. He wondered why Booth stood there silently, letting Prudence do all the talking.

"Cavendish is sending his decoy team back to ambush you and steal the gold. Then they'll hide it and Cavendish will resign from the mint eventually and claim it."

"Nice story," Fargo said. "But, I don't buy it. If Cavendish wanted to steal the gold, there would be lots of easier ways."

"Don't you see?" Pru said, angrily. "Matthew is saving the gold. He's taking it back to Denver City to the mint. Then people will believe him and he can clear his name. It's Paul Cavendish who is the crook. Matthew is innocent! He always was."

"And just how do you know that?" Fargo asked her, sarcasm sharp in his voice. "Because Booth told you so?"

"No," Prudence said.

"Then why?"

"Because he's my brother."

Fargo looked for a long moment from one to the other, from Pru's wide brown eyes to the deep dark eyes of Booth, and from her chestnut curls to his wavy dark hair.

"I see," he said. "Is that why you came west?"

"Matthew cabled me in Baltimore. He asked me to come to Denver City to help him clear his name. He never stole the gold from the mint when he was director. I know he didn't! He's a great man, like my father."

"Let me guess now," Fargo cut in. "Matthew found out about Paul Cavendish's plan. He knew we were carrying the gold. And he planned to follow me. But when the sheriff threw him out of town, he had no way of knowing when

139

we were leaving. So, you stayed to keep an eye on us."

"I'd do anything to help him," Pru said.

"So, now your dear brother plans to take this gold back to Denver City? With these fine upstanding men as escorts. Nice try, Booth," Fargo said.

"You don't believe him either?" Pru said, anger and pain in her face.

"Not a chance," Fargo answered.

"But it's true!"

"Then why are Sam and I tied up?"

Pru looked at him for a long moment, her face puzzled.

"Because you might be part of the plot," Booth answered smoothly. "You see, I'm not sure whether you were going to hide the gold for Cavendish to get later, or whether Wyatt Roundtree was going to double back and ambush you. Either way, I can't take any chances." Matthew Booth had a fast answer for everything, Fargo thought. He was slick.

Sam groaned. Pru rushed over and knelt beside him. "Sam?"

He didn't answer.

"He needs a cup of cold water," Fargo said. "Also, while you're down at the creek, pull up some of that green moss by the banks. Wash it real well and stuff it into those bullet holes, front and back."

Pru wrinkled her nose.

"It's an Indian remedy. Helps the wound close," Fargo said.

She nodded and disappeared.

"Pretty sister you got there," Fargo said to Booth as soon as she was out of earshot. "You must love her a lot, a whole lot, to send her out on the plains alone. Just to get yourself some gold."

Booth took several steps forward and stood over him. He reached down, grasped Fargo's neckerchief and pulled Fargo half to his knees, bending his dark face down close. Fargo felt his breath cut off for one long moment as he looked into the red fury blazing in Booth's face.

Booth let go, shoving him sideways onto the ground and then Fargo saw his leg pull back. He braced himself for the pain. The kick exploded agony between his legs. He doubled up, gritted his teeth and cursed Booth silently. He'd pay for this. He'd pay for all of this.

Fargo lay curled around himself, fighting the waves of pain and heard Booth walk away. After a while, Pru returned.

"Fargo! Are you alright?" she asked, seeing him lying on his side.

"Fine . . ." he gasped. "Just . . . resting . . . here."

She wouldn't believe him about Booth, he thought. The throbbing continued, radiating outward. He concentrated, pushing the pain away, thinking of Sam's shoulder. He could tell Pru was hesitant, unwilling to move the wounded man.

"You'll have to rip his shirt away," Fargo said between clenched teeth. "He'll groan, but do it anyway."

He heard her tentatively tearing the fabric.

"Don't be shy," Fargo said, the pain diminishing now. "Be sure to stuff moss deep down into the bullet hole. If Sam lives, he'll thank you for it."

He heard Pru gasping and panting as she did what she was told. When she had finished, she ran to the bushes and he heard the sound of dry retching. Fargo struggled to sit up, and inched his way back beside Sam. He looked at him carefully. Above his grizzled beard, Sam's cheeks were still ruddy. A good sign. While Fargo watched, Sam's eyes flickered open.

"Shit," he rasped.

"That sounds like a man who's going to make it," Fargo said.

Sam turned his face toward Fargo's.

"Can't feel my arm," he said, puzzled.

"Probably the way they got you tied," Fargo said.

"What kind of a pickle are we in?" Sam asked wearily, closing his eyes.

"A dilly," Fargo said. Sam's breathing slowed again as he fell back into unconcsciousness.

The four remaining bandits appeared, leading the mules and the two horses toward the wagon. The pig-eyed man who had shot Sam stepped on the chest of one of the dead men and the ribs cracked under his boot.

"Hey, listen to old Fox McNeil," he said, stepping on

the body again to break more ribs. "He's dead and he's still complaining." The other men laughed.

Booth and Prudence approached.

"Let's see what we got," Booth said to the men, gesturing to the wagon.

With a whoop, the four men boarded the wagon and began to throw off more of the gear, which rained down around Sam and Fargo.

"Sons of bitches! Careful with my stuff!" Fargo yelled, hoping to distract them. Hoping for a fight. Hoping to delay them until he could think of some way out.

"Shaddup," one of the men said, dropping an empty bucket on Fargo's head which glanced off leaving a white flash of pain. They knew what they were doing. They were looking for the gold.

"Bring down one of those wooden crates," Booth said. Two of the men lifted it out of the wagon and set it down before Booth. One of them fetched a pickaxe and Booth pried open the top. Inside were bags of canvas stamped "Auraria Private Mint, Denver City, Colorado Territory, United States of America."

Booth bent over and lifted one of the bags out of the crate with both hands. It was heavy. He loosened the drawstring at the top and turned it over, toward the ground. Out slid a long bar of dull-gray metal onto the grass. Skye's thoughts whirled. A lead bar. Not gold. Where was the gold?

Booth started and shot a sharp look at Fargo. He bent quickly, pulling up the bags and opening them, peering inside. From the look on his face, Fargo could tell there was no gold inside. The men could read Booth's face too.

"What the hell?" the pig-eyed man shouted. "Where's the gold you promised us?"

Skye saw Pru start and look toward Matthew Booth, her eyes wide with fear. So Booth had promised the men a share of the gold, Fargo thought. He had no intention of returning to the mint. And now Pru knew it too.

"Another box," he called, but the results were the same. Fargo could see Booth's face darkening to purple as his fury and frustration mounted.

Where was the gold? Paul Cavendish had double-tricked

them all, Skye thought with a flash of fury. Or maybe the decoy team was carrying the gold after all. No wonder Cavendish had been unconcerned that everyone in town seemed to know Fargo's mission. Cavendish wanted it that way. Cavendish had used Fargo to attract the conspirators. Skye felt his anger mount. Goddamn Paul Cavendish.

Booth was standing in front of him again.

"Where's the gold, Fargo?" he asked.

"Look, Booth. This is a surprise to me too. I thought we were carrying the real thing."

Booth's leg pulled back to kick him again and Fargo recoiled instinctively.

"No, Matthew!" Pru screamed.

"Stay out of this, Prudence," Booth said to her, his voice thick with rage.

"One more chance. Where's the gold?" Booth said.

"I told you. Cavendish packed those crates himself. I thought it was gold. Hell, it was heavy as gold . . ."

Fargo had a sudden thought and he fell silent. The bars were heavy. They could be solid lead. Or they could be gold. Painted or coated to look like lead. That would be just like Cavendish, he thought.

Booth was watching him carefully.

"You were saying, Fargo?" he muttered, nudging him with the toe of one boot.

"Said what I had to say."

"You're holding out on me," Booth said. "I can always tell when a man is holding out on me."

"I've told you what I know," Fargo said.

"But maybe less than you suspect," Booth added.

He drew his pistol and clicked open the chamber slowly, loading three bullets while watching Fargo. Then he held the pistol toward Fargo to show him.

"One bullet every other chamber," he said, clicking it shut and spinning it. "You a gambling man?"

"Not particularly," Fargo said.

"Let's play us a little game," Booth said.

"Matthew, please," Fargo heard the pain and disbelief in Pru's voice.

"Shut up!"

"Thanks, but no," Fargo said. "I don't like the odds."

"Well, I do," Booth said. "See this old man's knee-cap?"

He pointed the pistol at Sam's knee as he lay unconscious. Fargo twisted his bound hands for the hundredth time. Too tight. Couldn't get loose.

"Start talking or he's lost it," Booth said.

Fargo watched as Matthew Booth slowly cocked the pistol. He heard Pru whimpering in fear. Booth's finger tightened on the trigger.

"You win," Fargo said.

Booth relaxed slightly but still held the gun pointed at Sam's knee.

"Talk."

"I don't know for sure. It's just a suspicion," Fargo said. He hesitated. He hoped he wasn't right. At least it would buy them some time. "What if those are gold barss, but they're coated with lead?"

Booth shot a glance back toward the crate. "Interesting idea," he said. "How do we find out of it's true?"

"Try the fire," Fargo suggested. "Lead melts at a low temperature. Shouldn't take too long."

He doubted the lead would melt on the campfire. Not without somebody who would stick to the bellows and put up with hours of heat. But he kept his doubts to himself. Building up the fire would keep them busy. And it would keep him alive. For a while.

Maybe he could loosen his hands by then. He twisted them again. Didn't feel any looser, but he continued and could feel his wrists being rubbed raw.

"Build up the fire," Booth ordered the men. In a few minutes, they had a roaring fire going, the black smoke billowing skyward into the late afternoon sky. The men had found a cauldron in the wagon, which they suspended over the flames. Then they rifled through the wagon, carrying out the provisions, which they dragged over to the fire. They went through the bags and opened the tins, took a bite out of each and tossed the rest on the ground. Then they lounged about the fire while they waited for the lead to melt.

Fargo felt hunger gnaw at him but concentrated on his hands. He could feel the unmistakable warm wetness of blood on his wrists as he twisted them. And his hands were no looser.

He felt around behind him for a sharp corner on the rim of the wagon wheel. He finally located a rough spot at the edge of the iron and he began rubbing the rope back and forth, careful to keep his shoulders still so that no motion showed from the front. After ten minutes, he paused and felt the rubbed edges of the rope with his fingers. Only a few strands had been cut. At this rate, it would take all night. He kept at it. Prudence approached with a tin mug.

"Something to drink, Skye?" she asked, her voice shaky.

"Sure," he said gratefully. The water was cool and bracing. He felt a stab of hope go through him. He took two deep swallows and stopped. "Some for Sam. He needs it more than I do," he said to her.

He watched as Pru knelt and lifted the old man's head onto her knee. Sam stirred and Pru put the cup to his lips, pouring it gently into his mouth. Sam gulped a few times, swallowed, sputtered. Then he moaned and his head fell to one side again. Fargo saw Pru's eyes fill with tears.

"Help us," he said quietly to her.

"I can't," she said under her breath. "He's my brother. Besides, what can I do?"

"Bring me a knife. Any knife."

"You'll kill him!" she said.

"Not if I can help it," Fargo said. "I just want to get free. And get Sam and me outta here."

"I'll try," she said.

She moved toward the fire and sat down beside the open mess kit, glancing furtively around. She looked as guilty as hell, Fargo thought. She slipped her hand inside and then rose, drawing her shawl around her as she walked back toward him.

"Pru!" Booth called sharply. She hesitated, then stopped. "Where are you going?"

"They need some water . . . ." Pru said, suddenly aware that she no longer had the tin cup in hand.

"You gave them water already," he said impatiently. "Come over here."

Pru shot a desperate look at Fargo. She was too far away to toss the knife to him without detection.

145

"Damn," Fargo muttered to himself as she moved toward Booth.

Sam moaned and writhed uncomfortably. Pru glanced toward them.

"The old man might die," she said to Booth, pleadingly.

"Oh, alright," he muttered impatiently. Fargo held his breath as she approached. Behind her, Matthew Booth was watching warily. She slowly slid her hand down out of her shawl and dropped the knife beside Fargo's knee, trying to hide the motion behind her skirt. Fargo glanced down at it helplessly as she knelt beside Sam, and moved his leg slowly to cover the knife as it lay on the dirt. He felt Booth's dark eyes on him. Booth rose and walked toward them. Fargo shifted almost imperceptibly to make sure the hilt of the knife was completely hidden by his leg.

"Get up," Booth said to his sister.

"Let me help him," Pru said, continuing to minister to Sam.

"I said get up," Booth repeated, his voice hard-edged. Pru looked up at him in surprise.

"What is it, Matthew? Don't speak to me that way."

Booth leaned down and grasped her elbow, hauling her roughly to her feet. Then he suddenly kicked Fargo's knee where it lay over the knife. Pru screamed. Skye gritted his teeth, resisting the urge to move his leg, which would uncover the knife underneath. Booth leaned down and shoved Fargo's legs to one side to reveal the knife.

"Well, whaddya know?" Fargo said in mock surprise.

Booth cursed and kicked it away, far out of reach.

"I saw you take that knife," he said to Pru, spitting the words into her face and roughly shaking her. "You're just like all the others," he said. "You're part of the plot too."

"Ease up, Booth," Fargo said. "I made her do it."

"Matthew!" she said, her face pale and disbelieving. "Matthew! I'm on your side. I've helped you. But just let them go. I don't want to see anybody hurt."

"You're a fool then," he said. "I'm the one who's been hurt. My reputation has been ruined. I was the director of the mint. An important man. And what am I now?"

"Not much," Fargo said, enjoying the shades of purple

rising in Booth's face. It was a risky game to taunt a man with a gun when you were helpless, Fargo realized. But, if he could get Booth to make a mistake. Any mistake. Like stepping nearer.

"I'll have my revenge," Booth said, his voice controlled and low. He wasn't going to make a mistake, Fargo realized.

"Revenge?" she whispered.

"I'm going to make them pay," he said, drawing his revolver. "Every last one of them, starting with these two." He cocked the pistol and took slow aim.

Time halted as Fargo stared upward into the small dark hole of the barrel, with Matthew Booth's burning eyes on either side. Fargo noticed the way the silverwork on the gun glistened in the sun. He felt the grass under him, the hardness of the earth, the warmth of Sam nearby. He heard the old man's deep breath, and Pru's fearful panting, and the sharp click of the revolver being cocked. Then he became aware of another presence, a presence which crept forward unseen, a presence of subtle motion and sound.

Booth jerked forward, his eyes registering sudden surprise. A puzzled look came over his face and the pistol wavered, pointed upward and discharged, the bullet flying wide. Booth sank to his knees and fell forward across Fargo's legs, the red-and-brown feathered shaft of an Arapaho arrow sunk deep between his shoulder blades.

10

The air shattered with war cries. Fargo saw flashes of feathers and bare skin as the braves surged out of the brush toward the campfire. Two of Booth's men fell immediately, bristling with arrows. The other two retreated, firing wildly, and ducked behind a rock outcropping.

It was a small war party. He counted six. Young braves, Fargo noted, out to prove their manhood and avenge their tribe. The smoke from the fire had brought them. The Indians had hidden their horses and launched a surprise attack on foot.

He stayed still, watching the scene through half-closed eyes. Booth's body lay across him, the silver revolver still in his loosened grip. If only he could get his hands free. Again Fargo pulled on the ropes binding his hands, and cursed inwardly when they held fast. The knife. It lay on the dirt in front of him where Booth had kicked it. More than five yards away.

He heard a piercing cry and he looked up, under his lids. A brave had circled behind one of Booth's men and was raising his hatchet. The man turned and fired, catching the Indian and he slumped forward screaming his death cry. At the same moment, the man was shot by two arrows in the back. He stumbled and fell on top of the brave. There was only the pig-eyed man who had shot Sam. One man left. And not much time.

Pru had dropped to the ground, and lay shaking with fear beside Sam. The four of them looked like dead bodies, Fargo thought—himself propped against the wagon, Pru, Booth, and Sam on the ground. He hoped.

If they stayed still, they would be overlooked for the

moment, among all the dead bodies which littered the ground from the shootout. But when the fighting was over, and the braves began lifting the scalps . . . There was one slim chance. If he could only get his hands untied.

"Move very slowly," Fargo said quietly to Pru. "Get behind me, under the wagon. Untie my hands."

Pru did as she was told, wiggling bit by bit under the wagon. She didn't have far to go. He felt her fingers fumbling awkwardly at the ropes at his wrists. They weren't getting any looser.

"I can't do it, Skye," she whispered, her voice quaking. "The rope's too tight."

"Forget it," he said. It was futile. She was completely terrified and helpless. "Pull that canvas over you. Stay hidden. No matter what." He'd have to think of something else.

The pig-eyed man had panicked. He cowered between two large rocks, shooting, reloading, shooting. The braves danced around him, taking cover behind the rocks and brush, taunting him, shooting arrows close to him but aiming to miss. They were playing with him, Fargo thought, the way a badger fools with a wounded chipmunk. The braves began to close in, coming nearer. The man shot one of them in the chest as he sprinted from one rock to another. But then he raised his pistol, and it did not fire. The Indian whooped.

They did not shoot any more arrows. One of them advanced, a tall stocky brave with red beading on his breechcloth. The man clicked his empty pistol again and again in desperation. Finally, he threw it toward the brave, who ducked and raised a feathered hatchet above him. The man dropped to his knees as the Indian sank the hatchet deep into his skull, which caved in like an eggshell, the bloody mass inside oozing out onto the ground as the body hit the dirt.

It was over.

Fargo watched as the braves fanned out and began to examine the bodies of Booth's men, taking the revolvers, pulling off buttons, trying on hats and then discarding them. They did not take scalps from the bodies they had not killed.

He struggled again with the ropes binding his hands, but they held, cutting deeper into his wrists. There wasn't a hope in hell of wearing through the rope on the wheel rim. Not in time.

The Indian with the red-beaded breechcloth squatted down and wrenched his hatchet from the skull of the dead man. He grasped the hair with one hand, drew his knife with the other and carved off a large patch of the hair from above the forehead, tearing the scalp away from the skull.

Suddenly, one of the braves walked toward the wagon, heading staight for them. Fargo narrowed his eyes to slits. As the Indian drew nearer, Fargo watched, his eyes almost completely closed. He stilled his breathing. He felt a fly land on his face and crawl slowly across his cheek. He suppressed the urge to twitch. The beaded moccasins came nearer and nearer, until the brave stopped a few paces in front of Fargo.

There was a long quiet moment. Fargo felt the tickle of the fly on his face. And he felt the brave looking down at him, watching him carefully. The brave sensed he was alive. The game was up. There was nothing else to be done. Fargo opened his eyes and looked the Indian full in the face.

The brave was tall and muscled, his broad chest covered by a wide vest of narrow shells woven with rawhide. He carried himself with dignity, like a young chief. His hair hung long and loose behind him and an iridescent blue feather rose from the crown of his head. The warrior looked down, his face with its high, chiseled cheekbones and deep black eyes remained expressionless. He reached behind him slowly to remove an arrow from his quiver, fitting it to the bow and holding it easily in one hand, his eyes never leaving Fargo's.

He came nearer, warily. Then he drew the bow back slowly. Something was familiar about the brave. Fargo forced his mind to think clearly.

"Your words were wise," Fargo said in Algonquian.

The warrior started and looked at him closely.

"The mountains were white. You and your tribe went away from the place with cherries," Fargo said, remembering their meeting on the plains outside of Denver City.

"You are the white man who knew the ancient words of parting," the Indian said, lowering his bow.

Skye felt a small hope rise in him, dancing like the first flicker of a campfire. If he could nurse it along, keep it going.

His life depended on it. If he could keep the Indian's interest, keep talking . . .

"Another one alive, High Eagle?" Fargo heard an Indian voice say in Algonquian.

The large warrior with the red-beaded breechcloth approached and stood beside the first. From his belt hung his bloody tomahawk and the scalp of the pig-eyed man which dripped blood down the brave's muscled thigh.

"I have met this one before, Two Fists," High Eagle said. "He knows the ways of our people. He knows our words."

"Then he is an evil spirit," Two Fists said. The rest of the braves gathered in a semicircle to look down at Fargo.

"I do not think so," said High Eagle thoughtfully. "But he can tell us things. White man, how are you called?"

"Skye," he answered. "Like the color of my eyes." He opened them wide and rolled them about for the Indians to see. He would have to put on a good show or it would be his last. As he hoped, the braves leaned forward to look at his blue eyes, then muttered among themselves. Many Indians believed that blue eyes gave a man supernatural powers.

"Good name, good medicine," High Eagle said. "How do you come to know our words?"

"He is a trader! That is all. That is how he has learned our words." Two Fists said. "Many white men speak Indian tongues."

"But this one knows more than words," High Eagle insisted. "He knows our ways. He speaks as an Indian speaks."

"He is a white dog," Two Fists spit at him.

"I dreamed of this pale face," said High Eagle quietly, almost to himself. "It is good medicine to find him again. After we had words on the trail, I dreamed he flew above our camp, high overhead and looked down at us."

"I also dreamed," said Fargo, thinking quickly. He needed to produce some magic. That was what would keep him alive. "It was three nights ago," he continued. "I dreamed I flew above your camp in the night sky. I looked down and I saw an old man with a yellow headband who made the air dance with his hands. He sat in front of a tent with stripes. The fire was red and braves sat around him. He told how time began. A long story.''

"This is so!" one of the braves said. "Three nights ago!"

"He saw Speaks Long in his dream," said another excitedly.

"I say he lies!" Two Fists said. "I say, let us take his scalp. Leave him here for coyotes."

Two Fists bent down and wrenched the gun from Booth's hand. Fargo felt Booth's body twitch slightly as the gun was removed, and he wondered if Booth was still alive. Two Fists straightened and looked down at the carved silver work in the revolver.

"Watch the cowardice of white man," Two Fists said. "This will prove he is no Indian." He pointed the revolver straight at Fargo. Fargo remembered Booth loading the gun to shoot Sam's kneecap. A bullet every other chamber. And one bullet had discharged when Booth was shot by the arrow. Luck was with him. If he could only play it right.

"I will not die," Fargo said, smiling into the barrel.

Two Fists laughed and squeezed the trigger. The pistol clicked. Empty. His face darkened as the other Indians laughed, slapping their legs and each other. Clearly Two Fists was not well liked among the other braves, Fargo thought.

"The white man knows there is no death in this gun," Two Fists said angrily. "I still say he is a coward."

Two Fists turned the revolver toward his own face and looked down the barrel. Then he laughed defiantly and pulled the trigger. His face exploded, the blood spattering them all. He staggered backward and fell, contracted once, and then was still. The Arapaho warriors started at the unexpected sound of the shot, and drew closer together and exchanged looks among themselves.

Fargo felt the hope in him quicken. Luck had been with him. He had a chance. He had a good chance. But now, he had to get them all out alive. If he could keep a clear head. Look for an opening.

"You look at death and are not afraid," High Eagle said to Fargo. "You are not like any white man I have known. You will tell me things I want to know."

"I will answer your questions," said Fargo. Later he would ask for something in return.

"Why are white men on the warpath?" High Eagle asked.

"Crow took scalps up north," said Fargo. "Some white men do not see differences between tribes."

High Eagle considered his answer.

"Will all white men go on the warpath now?"

Fargo thought for a moment. He had to be careful. He didn't want to encourage the Arapaho to attack Denver City. On the other hand, he wanted them to leave him alone. What would make the Arapaho retreat? Maybe a bargain. If the Indians felt they had killed enough whites to avenge the unprovoked attack, they would stop fighting.

"The Arapaho are fierce warriors and fight like cougars," Fargo said. High Eagle did not smile at the flattery, but listened intently. "You made the white men who attacked you pay with their lives."

"This is so," High Eagle said.

"And the white men were weak. Bad warriors. You have killed more white men than they killed Arapaho," Fargo said.

High Eagle nodded again.

"There is no need to kill more. Other white men are peaceful," Fargo said. "They know the difference between Arapaho and Crow."

"He lies," another brave said.

High Eagle looked down at Fargo for a long time before he spoke and an expression like the memory of pain flickered across his face.

"We have heard this many times from the white man," High Eagle said, measuring his words. "But always it is the same. One white man says peace. Then other white men come to kill our women and children. Still other white men say now there will be peace. But there is no peace."

Fargo sighed. The Indian's words burned him like a branding iron. It was true. He had seen the Indians pushed off their lands, farther and farther west into land nobody else wanted. And then more settlers came and decided they did want it and the Indians fought and then moved again.

"Many times I do not understand white man either," he said.

"You speak as an Indian," High Eagle said.

"Part of me is," he answered. The braves whispered

153

among themselves and High Eagle nodded thoughtfully.

Just then, Sam groaned beside him. The braves started.

"The old one lives," one said.

"Let me take him," said another, stepping forward. He was a young boy, slender with bright eager eyes and carefully drawn sawtooth markings painted on his face and chest. He held his tomahawk tightly in his hand and from it hung the small body of a blackbird, stuffed and wound round with beaded cords as a good-luck charm. Fargo guessed it was the boy's first war party.

"There is no glory in taking a first enemy who is not fighting," said Fargo to the boy.

"That is right," said High Eagle. "This one belongs to a warrior who has already killed. Who will claim this old one's scalp?"

Fargo thought fast. "I claim all the ones left living," said Fargo, choosing his words carefully, but nodding only toward Sam.

"You claim?" High Eagle said with a laugh. "You lie here on the ground with your hands tied? By what right do you claim?"

"I have paid with my answers," said Fargo.

"That is true, Blue Skye," High Eagle said. "I grant you what you have asked."

One of the braves pulled Fargo to his feet and Booth rolled to one side. He moaned.

"The other lives!" a brave said. "It is High Eagle's arrow. So it is High Eagle's scalp."

High Eagle looked at Fargo.

"You are well named, clever one," High Eagle said. "The blue sky looks very plain like the wall of a new teepee. But we do not know what is behind it. All the living ones belong to you. I have spoken. So the old one is yours. And this one too, with my arrow in him."

Fargo smiled and nodded.

"Release his hands," High Eagle instructed. One of the braves cut the ropes and Fargo rubbed his raw wrists.

"Let us go," High Eagle commanded.

Just then the unmistakable sound of a sneeze came from beneath the wagon.

One of the braves started forward and pulled aside the canvas. Pru's terrified face looked up at him.

"Keep still if you want to live," Fargo said to Pru in English.

"A squaw too!" High Eagle said with astonishment. He laughed. "Are there any more alive?"

"That is all," Fargo said in Algonquian.

"Let us go before all the white men come back to life," High Eagle said. He raised his hand and the warriors began to walk away. Then he turned back to Fargo.

"Before I go, Blue Sky, I would like to know one thing more. I do not believe you dreamed. I do not believe you flew above our camp. That was my dream. I believe you came on foot in the night," High Eagle said. "This is what I heard behind your words."

"High Eagle sees what is behind the sky," Fargo said. The brave nodded.

"Then you move like air," High Eagle said with respect. "We will listen for you in the wind."

They exchanged the parting words solemnly and Fargo watched as the braves departed, the bleeding scalps dangling from their lances and their belts. They trotted away quickly and gracefully through the tall buffalo grass, carrying their dead with them.

Fargo stood looking after them in the silence.

Then he became aware of his surroundings again and he felt the familiar emptiness of other remembered battlefields, of the deserted killing places he had been. Fargo looked about at the bodies strewn on the grass, the wagon's gear lying in piles, the smoke of the fire still rising, unruly and black, into the clear air. He heard a shrill metallic whistling and his sharp eyes followed the sudden darting of a broad-tailed hummingbird, which paused above a mutilated body, then sped away. He heard the brook, the low gurgle of water in the stillness. Then Booth moaned, almost inaudibly, at his feet.

Fargo knelt. Matthew Booth lay on his side, the shaft of the arrow still protruding from between his shoulder blades, his shirt dark with the blood which seeped out around the shaft.

"Prudence!" Fargo said. He looked sharply at her still cowering beneath the wagon, her eyes wild, her face pasty white. She started at the sound of his voice, looking about her uncomprehendingly. He would have to snap her out of it. Fast.

"Prudence!" he said again, his voice hard. Her eyes focused on his face. "Come say good-bye to your brother."

She shook herself and crawled, as if asleep, from under the wagon. She was still shaking. When she saw Matthew's face, it seemed to bring her back.

"Matthew," she called. Booth moaned again, low in his throat.

Fargo moved aside and placed Booth's head gently on her lap, being careful not to move him much. The arrow was probably lodged next to his heart which was slowly hemorrhaging. It would be useless to remove the arrow, or even break off the shaft. It would cause the suffering man more pain and increase the bleeding.

"Prudence," Booth answered, the word low and slurred. "I was wrong . . . to get the gold . . . I thought if it was a secret . . . I would be successful." Booth paused a moment and swallowed. The words came with difficulty. "Cavendish was a success . . . I hated him for that. I wanted to be a success . . . even if I had to steal . . . to be important . . . like father."

Prudence's eyes widened, but she did not pull away from him.

"Don't talk now," she said. "That's all over."

"No . . . no . . ." he said. He took on the look of an old man, his face creased with the effort to speak. His lips moved before the words came.

"You were the only one . . . the only one who believed in me . . . and I lied to you—"

Booth's lips stopped moving and his eyes opened a little more. He looked surprised. Then the lines of pain on his face dissolved and the light left his eyes. Fargo reached over and closed the lids.

Fargo knelt beside Sam and put his hand on the old man's belly. His breathing was still deep and steady. Fargo pulled back the shirt and examined the wound. The moss was clean and had been pressed inside the wound. The bleeding had stopped, at least on the outside. But it would be several months, Fargo thought, before Sam would be panning for gold again.

Overhead, two black hawks wheeled in the late afternoon sky, floating in wide lazy circles. Fargo knew that they had their sharp eyes on the bodies lying below them. As long as there was movement below, they would not land. But their presence would bring on the turkey vultures, which wouldn't wait. He rifled through the wagon gear and found a couple of shovels.

Pru was still hunched over Booth's body, silent and still. Fargo put his hand on her shoulder and helped her to her feet. He took her arm, led her to the top of a low rise beneath a cottonwood nearby and handed her a shovel.

"Dig," he said. It would be the best thing for her, he thought. He knew that inside she was a confused mixture of grief and anger. They would dig graves all night long. The digging would help her work it out.

The eastern horizon was the pale blue of a robin's egg and the birds were atwitter in the brush. Fargo arose, stretched and washed up at the stream. He checked the livestock. The mules were still tethered where he left them. The Ovaro whinnied when it smelled him approaching. Pru's sorrel was nowhere in sight. But three of the horses from Booth's men stood grazing beside the others. Fargo picketed them. At the campsite, he gathered their supplies which had been scattered by the bandits.

Then he noticed the iron cauldron on three low rocks in the middle of the black ashes where they had built the fire the day before. He went over to look inside. The lead-colored bar lay at the bottom of the cauldon. So it hadn't melted in the heat after all. As he loaded the cauldron and the bar onto the wagon, he wondered if the bars were gold inside or lead straight through. Only one man knew for sure. And they would pay a visit to Paul Cavendish as soon as possible. Fargo was eager to be off. He hurriedly started a fire down by the creek and fixed a pot of coffee. Sam stirred.

"How's the shoulder?" asked Skye.

"Hurts powerful," Sam said.

"Can you move your arm?"

"Ouch! Sure can. But I don't want to."

"That's a healthy sign. We're breaking camp in a few minutes," Fargo said. "We're going to hightail it to Denver City. I've got some questions for Mr. Cavendish."

"Good morning, Skye," said Pru, rising and stretching. "How are you, Sam?" Her eyes had dark circles around them, but Fargo could tell from her voice that she would be fine.

"Got me the dagburndest hole in my old shoulder," Sam said. "And somebody done stuck some vegetation in there."

"I did that," Pru confessed.

"Did you now?" Sam asked, surprised. "Well that was a smart thing to do. You done saved Sam's whole shoulder. Not to mention the rest of him. Where'd you learn that old trick? It's an Indian thing."

"Skye told me how," she said looking up at Fargo.

"Figures," Sam said. "Speaking of Indians, I done had the dangblastedest dream. I've been lying there trying to piece it together. Seems this bunch of Indians . . ."

Fargo saw the stricken look on Pru's face.

"Later, Sam," he interrupted. "Later. Right now, let's get some breakfast in us."

After they ate, Pru disappeared and Fargo knew she had gone again to the hill where they had buried Matthew Booth and his men. While she was gone, Fargo told Sam briefly about Booth and the Indian attack.

"Daggummit!" Sam said. "Why'd I have to pass out in the middle of all the excitement?"

Fargo quickly finished loading the wagon, arranging the supplies so that there would be a place for Sam to lie down in the back on top of some soft sacks. He stacked the crates from the mint toward the rear of the wagon and covered them with canvas.

Then he hitched the mule team. The three strays were tethered in a line behind the wagon and the Ovaro was left running free to follow the wagon. When Pru returned from the hill, she climbed onto the driver's seat without a word and sat clutching her handkerchief.

"Hope we won't bounce you around too much," Fargo said as Sam settled onto the back of the wagon.

"I'm a tough old bird," Sam replied.

Fargo seized the reins and clucked to the mules. They stood still. He flapped the reins on their backs, but not one of them took a step forward.

"Get goin', you foul critters!" Sam called from the back of the wagon and, with a jerk, the team started forward.

Fargo headed northward along an overgrown track called Twisted Oak trail. This track met up eventually with the main eastern trail, the one the decoy team had taken. When they intersected the main trail, they would turn westward and take it into Denver City.

Fargo was guiding the wagon past a tall stand of gooseberry bushes when he saw a movement among the leaves. Someone, or more than one, was in the bushes. No horses were in sight. Might be Indians on foot, he thought. He pressed the reins into Pru's hands and eased the Colt out of his holster.

As they drew near, a man crashed out of the bushes and ran into the middle of the track, holding his hands high to stop the wagon. Fargo raised his pistol and looked about, expecting an ambush. The man was disheveled, his clothes filthy and torn, his forehead smeared with dirt and dried blood. Then Fargo recognized the brown-bearded man who had led the vigilantes out of Denver City to attack the Arapaho. It was Budge Hays. Fargo swore.

"Stop! Stop!" Hays said. "We need help!"

Fargo grabbed the reins from Pru and halted the wagon.

"What the hell?" Fargo said.

"Me and my friends got attacked by Indians," Hays said.

"You got attacked?" Fargo scoffed.

Then Hays looked again at Fargo. "Hey, don't I know you?" he asked suspiciously.

"Yeah," Fargo said. "And I know you, Budge Hays. I know you went after those Arapaho even when I told you it was Crow that killed those settlers. I also know the Arapaho came after us because of your attack. What ever you got from them Indians in return wasn't enough if you're still standing here. You're getting no help from me."

Budge sputtered with rage.

"Look you. I got two friends in the bushes hurt real bad. We lost our horses and our guns in the fight. There's Indians all over the place. We need to get back to Denver City. You'd better give us a ride . . .."

"Or what?" Fargo said. He slapped the reins down across the mule team and they moved forward a few paces. Budge stamped the ground in rage.

"Goddamn it! You can't leave us here in the middle of Indian territory. We're being hunted. This is murder!"

"This is justice," Fargo said. Just then a moan came from the gooseberry bush. One man staggered out, supporting himself with a crooked branch, dragging a busted leg behind him. Another man crawled out from underneath the branches. He had been scalped, the hair sliced away from half of his skull and dried blood blackened his face and neck. Pru clutched Fargo's arm.

"That man ought to be dead," she whispered.

"A man can survive a scalping," Fargo said. "But, as far as I'm concerned, all three of them deserve to be dead."

"You going to leave us here?" Budge Hays asked.

Fargo pulled up on the mules and brought the team to a halt again. He shouldn't do this, he told himself. They didn't deserve it. But one thing was certain. He was not going to travel with these vigilantes. High Eagle had let him off with his life. But if the Arapaho caught up to him again in the company of the men who had attacked the Indian camp, he wouldn't be so lucky a second time.

"Take the three horses tied to the back of the wagon," Fargo said. "Not the loose pinto, the other three."

Fargo watched as Hays walked to the back of the wagon. Just as he was untying the lead horse, a gust of breeze blew the canvas on the wagon. Fargo saw Hays look into the wagon, do a double take and then glance up at him, a dark glitter in his eyes. He wondered what Hays had seen. Then Hays led the horses to the front of the wagon.

"There's a price on the horses, Hays," Fargo said.

"Oh, yeah?" Hays said, his tone nasty and defiant now that he had his hands on the horses' bridles.

"Yeah. Keep your stinking face out of my sight. Next time

I see you, I'll shoot," Fargo said, his voice edged with a sharp knife. The three men mounted. The lame one had to try several times.

"Next time I see you, Mister Skye Fargo, you'll be hanging," Hays shouted back as the men galloped off.

Fargo watched the dust ball ahead of them diminish gradually as they rode out of sight.

"Hanging. What the hell did he mean by that?" Sam said.

The breeze blew another gust and Fargo heard the canvas flapping. He got down and went to the back of the wagon. The canvas had come loose and was blown back to reveal the crates from the mint. On top was one Booth had pried open. Inside the crate Fargo could see the canvas bags labelled Auraria Private Mint and clearly holding ingots. That was what Hays had seen. Of course, Hays thought it was gold, Fargo thought wryly. Well, hell. What if he did? What could Hays do to him? Cavendish knew the real story. And once they were back in Denver City, Paul Cavendish would have a lot of explaining to do.

Fargo secured the canvas and climbed into the wagon again.

"Too bad the Arapaho didn't finish 'em off," Sam remarked.

"Maybe I should have just left them here," Fargo muttered, half to himself.

"No," Pru said. "You did the right thing."

Ahead, Fargo saw the trail wind through the low square buildings of the ghost town called Twisted Oak. The town had started going downhill when the main stagecoach line was established a few miles north and, a few years later, everybody had gone to live someplace else. But the board buildings remained, blank windowed and deserted in the mid-afternoon heat.

As they drove down the dusty main street, Fargo heard the banging of a shutter in the wind. Pru huddled closer to him.

"Gallopin' ghosts! What a spooky place," she said.

He nodded agreement and looked up and down the empty streets. Nothing moved except a small tumbleweed rolling down the street. His sixth sense told him that something wasn't right.

"Get down!" he shouted at Pru, pushing her off the seat and into the back of the wagon at the same instant that the shot exploded and the wood splintered on the seat next to him. In one fast motion he slapped the mule team into action and drew his Colt, aiming at an empty window with broken glass, where he guessed the shot came from. He saw a movement in the window and he fired, but whoever it was drew back in time. Gunfire erupted from several directions.

The team was pulling hard. Fargo saw an alleyway ahead. That would give them some cover. A shot zinged by his ear from behind and Pru screamed. Fargo turned in his seat instantly and fired at the man standing on the rooftop. He clutched his chest and fell forward, as if in slow motion onto the street where he lay motionless. The wagon careened around the sharp corner into the alley and came to a stop. Fargo leapt down, reloading and moving warily toward the street, his Colt out in front of him, keeping his back to the wall.

"I'll cover you," Sam said. He was propped up in the back of the wagon, holding his rifle braced against his knees. Fargo crept to the edge of the building and removed his hat. He tossed it out onto the street and a barrage of gunfire made it dance across the dust. Fargo watched the hat carefully. There were at least a dozen men. A dozen shooting at his hat anyway. There might be more. And they had taken up positions in all directions.

He cursed under his breath.

He looked down and saw that a part of the wooden skirting on the side of the building had rotted and fallen. He could see underneath the building and he ducked down to look. There was a crawl space which led all the way along the street under the floorboards and the high boardwalk. He might be able to make his way down to the end of the street and pop up where they weren't looking for him.

"Make some noise for a while, Sam," Fargo said.

"Yup," Sam answered. He began shooting out of the alleyway, at windows across the street. As Fargo crawled through the hole and under the building, he hoped none of the snipers had a fix on Sam. The dust was terrible and he suppressed the desire to sneeze as he wriggled through the dirt beneath the boardwalk, inching around the support beams sunk into the earth. There was enough light filtering in between the warped boards that he could see his way. He listened to the occasional pop of gunfire as he crawled toward a distant patch of light.

Some missing stairs on a corner of the boardwalk gave him a clear view of the street from the other end. Across the way, Fargo saw a gunman crouching behind a barrel, looking toward the alleyway where he had driven the wagon.

Beyond the sniper, in a stable yard, Fargo saw the three horses he had given to Budge Hays. So Hays was here. Hays had something to do with this ambush. He cursed and then cursed again. That would teach him to be generous, he thought and his fingers twisted with the desire to get his hands on Budge Hays. But who were the other men?

Fargo eased himself out of the hole in the stairway, keeping an eye on the gunman who was intently watching the other end of the street. Then, Fargo backed away toward the corner of the building for cover. When he reached it, he turned and ran straight into Budge Hays.

Hays yelled and turned white. He fumbled with his gun, his hand shaking, clearly terrified. Fargo grabbed Hays around the neck and pulled him against the wall, jamming the barrel of his Colt against Hays's neck. Hays was shaking like a leaf.

"Drop it," he said. Hays dropped the gun on the street. "Kick it," Fargo said. He did, but not very far. "Talk."

"You'll hang for this, Fargo," Hays hissed.

"Hang for what?" Fargo asked.

"Stealing gold from the mint," Hays replied. "I saw it in your wagon."

Fargo laughed, a short humorless bark.

"So, that's it? Always going after the bad guys are you, Hays? Only you go after the wrong ones. But you shoot first. Find out later. That how you do it?" Fargo pushed him roughly away and Hays dove for his gun, fumbling as he landed on it. A shot sounded and Fargo saw Hays's body recoil. His gun had gone off under him. Hays groaned, twitched, and then lay still.

"Freeze!" Fargo heard a man call out. Two men appeared on the rooftop above him, and three more at windows across the street. Every one of them had a gun pointed straight at him. The odds were impossible. Fargo tossed his gun onto the ground and raised his hands slowly.

Walking toward him up the street, Fargo saw Wyatt Roundtree leading several of the men from the decoy team, who had their pistols drawn and were covering him. Wyatt was walking slowly, his chest out and a slight swagger in his gait.

"Wyatt!" Fargo said. "What's going on here? You ought to be in Kansas by now."

Wyatt looked Fargo up and down slowly. He stopped by the body of Budge Hays and nudged it with the toe of his boot. Hays was dead.

"We would be in Kansas if it weren't for your dirty little trick," Wyatt said, his voice edged with excitement which he fought to control. "I don't know how you pulled it off, but I've caught you at it. Hand over the gold, Fargo."

"You have the gold, Wyatt."

"Don't play games with me, Fargo. Hays told me he saw it in your wagon."

"He saw some bags from the mint. That's all," Fargo said firmly. Wyatt's eyebrows raised. Fargo pressed on. "But why aren't you halfway through Kansas with the gold shipment?"

"We were crossing a gulch. One of the crates fell off and split open. Then we discovered somebody switched the gold ingots for lead bars. We were headed back to Denver City to find out what was going on."

"And you ran into Hays," Fargo said. Wyatt nodded. "And Hays told you I had gold in the back of my wagon."

"Lucky break for us," said Wyatt. "Caught you red-handed. I thought there was something funny the first time I met you."

"So you were going to catch me and take me back to Cavendish. With the gold."

"Exactly."

"And be the big hero." Fargo laughed and Wyatt flushed.

"What of it, Fargo?"

"Well, I hate to disappoint you, but Paul Cavendish hired me too. Told me I was carrying the real gold and you were the decoy. Only, I found out I'm carrying the same lead bars you are. Go check the wagon if you don't believe me."

Wyatt started. "Then where is the gold?"

"Only one man knows for sure," Fargo said. "Let's go find out."

Fargo shoved aside the guard and kicked open the office door. Cavendish jumped to his feet, his hands on the desk before him.

"What the hell's going on?" Fargo said. He entered the office followed by Sam leaning heavily on Wyatt Roundtree.

"What happened?" Cavendish said, seeing Sam's blood-stained shirt. "Should I call Doc Fletcher?"

"Nah," Sam said. "I'll hold out for a while."

"Meanwhile, I've got questions," Fargo said. "We all do."

"Get out and close the door," Cavendish said sharply to the guard who had recovered his wits and had followed them in. "Now, sit down and tell me what happened," he said to the three of them.

"No!" said Fargo. He crossed the room and threw the heavy lead ingot down onto the desk blotter. "You talk, Cavendish. You tell us what happened. We've been out there risking our necks and we find out we're carrying this. What is it? Where's the gold?"

"Right here," Cavendish said, patting the safe behind him.

"So you sent us both out as decoys," Fargo said, his eyes narrowing. "Thanks a lot for telling me."

"But, Mr. Cavendish," Wyatt said, "you told me I was supposed to carry the gold all the way to Philadelphia . . . ."

"Shut up, kid," Fargo muttered and Wyatt fell silent. "Last time we talked, you told me Wyatt was supposed to draw off the conspirators while we slipped the real stuff through. What happened to the plan?"

"I'm sorry, Skye. I thought I should take out an extra insurance policy," Cavendish said.

"Us," Fargo said. "Sam and me."

"Yes," Cavendish admitted. "You see, I could trust no one. Not even you. I knew Booth would suspect that there would be a trick. I knew he'd be smart enough to nose around and find out our real plans. So I decided to let it be known that you and Sam were carrying the gold. I was the only one who knew that the gold was right here. I had to do it that way."

"Can't keep a secret in Denver City," Sam said, nodding.

"Exactly," Paul said. "I suspected Booth would try to follow you. From the look of that blood on Sam's shirt, I guess he caught up with you. Where is he now?"

"Left him six feet under a cottonwood, along with thirteen of his men," Fargo said.

Cavendish whistled softly.

"They were fighting mad to find those bars were gray and not yellow," Fargo added. "Luckily, some Arapaho came by."

Cavendish whistled again.

"If I'd known about the Indians in advance and that Booth would find that many cohorts, I'd have sent some more men off prospecting with you," Paul said. "Believe me, if I could have told you, I would have. But I couldn't trust anyone."

"That's a lame excuse for putting our lives on the line," Fargo muttered.

"If you knew Booth was the conspirator . . ." Sam began.

"Why didn't I just accuse him?" Cavendish asked. "I couldn't. You see, some people here would say it was a witch hunt, some kind of revenge for that trick Booth pulled here when he was director of the mint. Some people still think he was innocent."

"We found out Booth had the theft planned all along," Fargo said. "Booth was mad you'd been such a success here. He wanted you to fail. And he wanted gold."

"I thought as much," Cavendish said. "I had a scare the day before you and Sam left, when the sheriff threw Booth out of town for reckless riding. If he wasn't in town, he couldn't find out which way you'd gone. How did he manage to track you?"

"He sent his sister after us," Fargo said.

"Sister?"

"Prudence. Prudence Booth. She came out west to help her brother."

"Interesting," Cavendish remarked. "That explains her sudden interest in me when she discovered I was connected with the mint. And why she was so eager to get a job here. Well, that about ties it up. Now that we've flushed out the conspirators, I'd like for you to leave tomorrow, Wyatt. This time, you'll be carrying the gold. I promise."

"Yes sir," Wyatt answered. "I'll let my men know. We'll leave first thing in the morning," Wyatt got up to depart and then turned back. "Mr. Fargo," he said, extending his hand. "Sorry, I misjudged you. Maybe I have some things to learn," he said, ducking his head and leaving.

"You ready for a week's relaxation? On me?" Paul asked.

He turned toward the safe, dialled the combination and opened the heavy door. Inside Fargo saw the bags of gold dust on the bottom shelf and the piles of coins and currency at the top. Cavendish removed two leather purses and tossed them onto the desk. They clinked promisingly.

"I would say you and Sam were some of the best insurance this mint ever had," he said, pushing the leather bags across the table toward them. Fargo rose to his feet and walked to the safe. He reached inside and removed three more bags of coins. Cavendish raised a hand in protest, then thought better of it.

"That one," said Fargo, tossing the first onto the desk in front of the old prospector, "is for the hole in Sam's shoulder." Cavendish nodded meekly. "And these two are for not telling us the truth." Fargo tucked one inside his shirt and pitched the other toward Sam.

"Hell, this'll keep me in mules and tools for the rest of my natural life," Sam said, his eyes glittering. "I can do what I've always wanted."

"What's that?" Fargo asked.

"Pan for gold," Sam said, "for the fun of it."

"One final question, Cavendish," Fargo said. "Who was your source? You told me you knew the conspirators from a lady. But you wouldn't say who."

There was a knock at the door and Cavendish called out to enter.

Fanny's round face appeared, followed by the rest of her curves as she bustled into the room.

"Welcome back, Fargo. Sam." Fanny said, her broad smile crinkling her sparkling eyes. "I heard you rode into town with Sam all bloodied up. Doc Fletcher will be right along. I guess you ran into Booth."

"There's my source," Cavendish said.

"You bet," she admitted. "Matthew Booth planned the whole thing in my saloon. You wouldn't believe the things me and my girls hear as we're waiting tables! Just don't tell anybody it was me."

"Why the big secret?" Sam asked.

"Bad for business," Fanny said. "It would be a disaster if folks realized me and my girls know every secret in town. First people would stop talking in my saloon. Then they'd stop coming!"

The three men laughed.

"Speaking of my establishment," Fanny said, "there's someone waiting for you over there." She looked meaningfully at Skye, her eyebrows raised.

"Guess I'd better go over and see who it is," Fargo said nonchalantly and headed for the door. Outside, an early summer rain was beginning to spatter the dusty street. On the way he spotted Pru in front of the stagecoach office, her parasol above her head. A stagecoach was loading. She looked relieved when she saw him.

"Skye!" She threw her arms around him. "I was hoping you'd come by. I'm leaving Denver City."

"Why?"

"Because if I stayed, every place I went I would think of Matthew. Everybody would know I'm Matthew's sister. I want my own life."

"Going back to Baltimore?"

"No, I left there for good. I'm staying out west."

Fargo laughed. "Aren't you the girl who said Denver City was a holy hellhole?"

"Well, I did," she admitted. "But the west has kinda grown on me. I'm going to try Dodge City. Where are you going, Skye? I mean . . . after Denver City?'' He heard the longing in her voice.

"Here. There," he said. "I'm not the settling type."

She nodded. He had answered her unspoken question.

"I thought not," she said. "But look me up if you're ever . . ."

"Get on board," the driver said.

Pru looked up at Fargo searchingly. "Thank you, Skye," she said, her eyes filling with tears. She could say no more. One of the passengers helped her inside and the coach pulled away. Fargo turned to watch as she waved good-bye, her face at the stagecoach window, as he had first seen her.

Laurel lay with her head on him, her long silken tresses a waterfall cascading across and down his chest. Her breathing was soft and deep as she dozed. Rain drummed its fingers on the tin roof. Fargo gazed up at the blank ceiling, thinking of the wide plains, the mountain peaks, the vast lands that lay all around the towns men had built in the wilderness. He felt the pull of the places he had never been, and of the places he hadn't seen for a while, half-remembered faces, promises kept, trails broken.

She stirred, warm against him.

"Skye . . ." she murmured.

He glanced down at her delicate beauty, her pale creamy skin and long limbs wound among the sheets.

"Hmmm?"

"Will you be staying long?"

"A little while. Until something comes up," he answered.

She moved against him, awakening slowly.

"Something always come up," he said.

She giggled when she saw what he meant.

LOOKING FORWARD!

**The following is the opening
section from the next novel in the exciting
Trailsman series from Signet:**

THE TRAILSMAN #127
NEVADA WARPATH

*1860, Utah Territory, where mutual hatreds
spilled over into the bloody Paiute War,
and not even the Pony Express
could get through . . .*

The big man astride the splendid pinto stallion reined up in
alarm and stared at the smoke rising skyward to the south. His
lake-blue eyes narrowed as he deciphered the message. Smoke
signals were much like Morse code and were used to relay
a wide variety of information. In this case, the warrior doing
the signaling was telling the other members of his tribe that
a lone white man was riding due west. Clearly, the warrior
hoped his tribesmen would stop the rider.

Skye Fargo relaxed slightly. Since he was heading south-
west, the smoke did not apply to him. But it meant another
man was in trouble, or soon would be, and might need some
help. Without hesitation he spurred the Ovaro into a gallop
and rode hard toward the low, narrow ridge from which the
smoke rose. The rider would be visible from up there, and
he could decide whether to go to the man's aid or not.

He crossed an alkali flat to reach the ridge, using the mes-
quite and scraggly pines for cover as much as possible. The

gradual slope was barren and he went up in a rush, drawing his Colt as he neared the rim. He reached the top exactly where he wanted to be—as close to the source of the signal as possible. Which turned out to be within twenty yards of a lone brave on his knees beside a small fire, a damp blanket clutched in his hands.

From the Indian's near-naked appearance and shaggy hair, Fargo recognized at a glance that the man was a Paiute. Back in Salt Lake City he'd been warned the Paiutes were on the warpath, and a friendly bartender had advised him to put off traveling to California until after the hostilities ended. But Fargo had pressed on, preferring to rely on the skills he had honed during his life on the frontier to keep him out of trouble, rather than wait weeks or even months until the Paiutes were defeated.

The brave took one look at the big man in buckskins and let the blanket fall onto the fire. Twisting, he grabbed a bow lying next to his left leg and notched an arrow to the string in a smooth motion. The barbed tip swung up and around and he began to draw back on the string.

Fargo fired a single shot that struck the Paiute squarely in the center of the forehead and knocked him onto his back, his arms out flung. Stopping near the fire, Fargo saw the smoldering blanket, then raised his gaze to scan the country beyond the ridge. Right away he saw the other rider, a figure in buckskins about a half mile distant who was galloping hell-bent for leather toward a wash. And well he should, because in bloodthirsty pursuit were five Paiutes on their lean war ponies.

Holstering his Colt, Skye moved to the southern edge and anxiously watched the grim tableau unfolding below. He was too far off to be of any help, and from the look of things, the other man was going to escape unscathed. Already the lean figure enjoyed a commanding lead and his sturdy mount gained ground with every stride.

Suddenly, just as the rider was almost to the wash, his horse buckled and went down. The man leaped clear over his animal's head, stumbled, and fell to his knees. Then, rising, he drew a pistol and pivoted to face the charging warriors.

"Damn," Fargo muttered, and went down the ridge in a swirling cloud of dust. Angling toward the rider, he slipped his big Sharps from its holster and held it in his right hand. The intervening brush prevented him from observing the fight. He heard shots and whoops and hoped the man could hold out until he got there.

When still over two hundred yards away, Fargo skirted a thicket and found himself in the open with a clear view of the Indians and the rider. The man had fallen and was surrounded by four mounted braves. The fifth stood over their victim and was taking aim with an arrow. All five were armed with bows.

Fargo whipped the Sharps to his shoulder, but before he could squeeze the trigger, he saw the fifth brave send the shaft into the downed man's abdomen. Scowling in anger, he released the reins and rode by the pressure of his thighs and legs alone, freeing his hands to shoot. Trying to sight while at a full gallop was difficult and only the best marksmen could do it, yet he barely hesitated as he took a bead and fired.

Two hundred yards distant the fifth Paiute threw up his hands and collapsed. Immediately the rest turned toward the source of the shot, vented whoops of fury, and urged their ponies to the attack.

Fargo fed another round into the chamber, sighted on the foremost Paiute, and fired again. The blast of the powerful gun rolled off across the plain and the Paiute pitched head first to the hard earth.

The remaining three swerved to the east, making for a stand of trees. Their bows were no match for the newcomer's deadly rifle and they well knew it. They were still a score of yards from safety when a third shot toppled a third brave, and once the surviving pair reached the trees they kept on going. Revenge on the whites was one thing, certain suicide quite another.

Skye slowed as he neared the hapless rider. There were two arrows protruding from the man's stomach. Such shafts, tipped as they were with barbed points that tore a man's insides as as a bullet, often caused a lingering, exquisitely painful death. And frequently Indians dipped their arrows in rattlesnake venom or the livers of dead animals, so any puncture would spread poison into the system, making the shafts even more lethal.

He held no hope for the rider, although the man's right arm was moving feebly. The horse had tripped in a shallow hollow and broken a leg. It lay on its side, breathing heavily, its eyes wide with fright.

The rider turned his head at the sound of the Ovaro's hoofs and looked up, his youthful features etched with acute agony. Relief temporarily replaced the torment when he realized it was a white man and not the Paiutes. He licked his thin lips, then croaked out, "Need . . . help."

Fargo glanced at the trees to make sure the war party had gone, then swung to the ground and crouched next to the young man. Closer inspection verified his earlier assessment. Both arrows were in deep and the man's buckskin shirt was soaked with blood. "There's not much I can do for you," he admitted softly.

The man nodded. "I know," he said, his voice weak. A trickle of blood formed at the corner of his mouth.

"Would you care for some water?" Fargo asked.

"No," the young man replied. "Need help."

Fargo thought the man must be in shock. He'd just told him there was nothing he could do. "There's no doctor for hundreds of miles," he said. "And if I try to take out those arrows you'll bleed faster and die sooner."

The rider gave a slight shake of his head and grimaced. "Not me. The mail."

"The what?" Fargo asked, wondering if he had heard correctly.

"The mail. Get it to the next station."

Fargo looked at the stricken horse again and blinked in surprise. He should have seen it sooner. The animal was fitted with a unique saddle few men had ever straddled: the distinctive, lightweight, stripped-down kind used exclusively by an outfit that had only been in business slightly over a month. And draped over the saddle was a leather rectangle known as a *mochila* with a mail pouch called a *cantina* at each corner. "You ride for the Pony Express," he declared.

"Yes," the rider said.

Stories about the fledgling mail service were in all the newspapers and being discussed in every saloon and around every campfire in the West. Started by the freighting firm of Russell, Majors, and Waddell, the Pony Express was a bold enterprise being conducted on a grand scale. A chain of riders now carried the mail from St. Joseph, Missouri, to San Francisco in less than half the time required before the Express, as it was frequently dubbed, went into operation.

"Will you take it, mister?"

The question gave Skye pause. He wasn't an Express employee and wasn't obligated in any respect to complete the rider's run. But as he gazed at the young man's earnest expression and saw the silent appeal in the man's eyes, he had a change of heart.

All that he had heard about the Express riders flashed through his mind. They were all close to twenty years of age and lightly built. They were all tough and resilient and expert horsemen. Above all, they were all committed to the oath of loyalty they were required to take—a pledge of honesty and proper conduct.

"Please," the rider said.

Skye glanced at the *mochila*.

"The mail must go through," the young man stated, repeating the company slogan in a tone that made his statement an entreaty. "Please, mister."

"All right," Fargo agreed, wondering what he had let himself in for. "I'll take the mail to the next station."

A smile of gratitude creased the young man's lips. "Thanks. The next stop is Roberts Creek."

"What's your name?" Fargo asked. The words were no sooner spoken than the rider gasped, stiffened, and went limp. He put a hand on the man's wrist and felt for a pulse. There was none.

Sighing, Fargo stood and replaced the spent rounds in his rifle and the Colt. Roberts Creek wasn't all that far—perhaps ten miles all told—so dropping off the mail wouldn't entail much of a delay. He twirled the revolver into his holster, slid the Sharps into its saddlecase, and stepped to the Express horse.

The animal looked up at him and whinnied. A jagged piece of bone jutted from the torn flesh on its front leg.

Fargo leaned down and stripped the *mochila* off. He knelt and stroked the animal's neck, putting the horse at ease. In a minute, the animal placed its head on the ground and wearily closed its eyes. Only then did Fargo ease the Çolt out, touch the tip of the barrel to the gelding's forehead, and shoot. The horse barely quivered and was still.

"You deserved better," Fargo said softly, and stood. In a land where a man's life frequently depended on his mount, he appreciated a good horse as much as anyone. And the animals used by the Express were the best money could buy.

He carried the *mochila* to the Ovaro, then folded it in half and draped it on his saddle behind the cantle. Taking a length of rope from his saddlebags that he normally used when picketing the stallion, he tied the *mochila* securely.

A shadow flitted across the ground nearby. Fargo pushed his hat back and glanced skyward. Already circling far overhead was a solitary buzzard. Given time, more would join it. He debated whether to bury the Pony Express rider and decided against it. In the first place he didn't have anything to dig with, and in the second place, the Paiutes might get the notion to swing around and try their luck again.

Reluctantly, he climbed onto the stallion and headed out, riding due west. In short order he crossed the wash and went a mile over a dry flat. The heat was like an oven, and the ground reflected its waves. Sweat trickled down his back.

As he rode he was constantly alert. Where there were five Paiutes, there might well be more, and that smoke signal was bound to attract others. The Paiutes had never been regarded as an especially fierce tribe, but desperation had driven them to extreme measures.

Always among the poorest of tribes, the Paiutes subsisted on whatever the harsh land had to offer, which wasn't much. In the winter, they lived on a meager diet of small game. In early spring, they ate the first fresh plants, particularly cattails, which the women gathered by the hundreds. Through the rest of the spring and summer they hunted ducks, caught fish, and collected wild rice. Come the fall, their diet changed to pine nuts and rabbit meat. They never had a surplus of food and often went hungry for days at a time.

Then along came the white man. As usual, the whites had little regard for the natives and treated them with disdain. The whites hunted and fished to their hearts' content, taking a large portion of what little food the land had to offer for themselves. The Paiutes found themselves in competition with hordes of migrating whites and didn't like it one bit. To the whites it was a matter of filling their bellies on their way west. To the Paiutes it was a matter of tribal survival.

The last straw, or so Skye had heard, came when the whites took to hacking down pinon trees for wood—the very trees the Paiutes depended on for their nuts in the fall. On top of that, the previous winter had been bitterly cold with many fierce blizzards. The Paiutes suffered terribly, and they blamed all of their suffering on the white man.

So, recently, war had erupted, and so far the Paiutes were holding their own. They had raided a number of Express stations, remote ranches and isolated communities, slaying dozens before the whites even realized the Paiutes were on the warpath.

Then came the disastrous battle of Pyramid Lake. A volunteer force of one-hundred and five men recruited from Carson City, Virginia City, Genoa, and other towns, assembled and marched out to punish the Paiutes for their transgressions. Unfortunately, because they viewed the Indians with contempt, they marched boldly up to a Paiute encampment at Pyramid Lake and into as perfect a trap as was ever conceived by any Indians anywhere. Almost half of the whites were slain before the rest fled in panic. Later, the Paiutes would say that many of the white men cried like little papooses as the warriors swarmed among them and were as easy to run down and kill as cattle.

Fargo had been told in Salt Lake City that a new effort was soon to be mounted against the Paiutes. This one would be better organized and be led by an experienced military officer. But until then, any white man or woman venturing west of Salt Lake City did so with no guarantee they would ever arrive in California.

A drumming noise from the rear shattered Skye's reflection. He looked back over his shoulder to see the pair of Paiutes who had gotten away earlier, and twenty of their furious tribesmen rushing to overtake him.